FOREVER YOURS THIS NEW YEAR'S NIGHT

STAR LIGHT ~ STAR BRIGHT SERIES BOOK TWO

L. A. SARTOR

eISBN: 978-0-9856792-6-2
ISBN: 978-0-9856792-7-9

Cover art: Copyright © L.A. Sartor 2014
Printed in the United States of America

www.lesliesartor.com

Star Light, Star Bright
The first star I see tonight,
I wish I may, I wish I might,
Have the wish I wish tonight.

~ anonymous

For my mom, Mary Sartor, who has forever believed in me, telling me I could do anything. You've never held me back, always letting me soar to the highest of stars. I love you.

And always for my husband Gary, who makes it possible for me to play with my characters and create a world for them. I love you.

1

_____

"WE HAVE MET, I'M WOUNDED YOU DON'T REMEMBER."

Jennifer Malone looked up from her bowl of fettuccine Alfredo. The same man who'd fed her that lame "haven't we met" pickup line while she was waiting in the bar for her table, had returned. "I thought I made it fairly clear I wasn't interested."

He stood way too close to her chair for comfort. She dropped her gaze, not wanting to lead him on. Damn, dining alone shouldn't make her a target for his advances. Especially not in this elegant restaurant high above Washington, DC.

"Are you still a sore loser, or is it that you really don't remember me?"

Pulling her thoughts together, Jen looked put down her fork and looked closely at the man in front of her. Tall, dark and way too handsome, this guy was someone she wouldn't have easily forgotten. His gray eyes held the hint of a private joke, his lips curving up on one side as if amused by their encounter.

A shadow of a name passed her mind, but no way could he be the same person.

She squinted and realized with a sick jolt that, although he wore his hair longer and had a five o'clock shadow most movie stars would envy, he was the same man.

Major Brice Young, who was a major jerk. She smiled at her own pun, then quickly put on her serious game face.

"Regrettably, I recall our last meeting all too clearly." She put as much displeasure as she could into those three words. *That should do it.*

Instead, he laughed, taking her off guard. Most men would have taken the hint and left her alone the first time she'd brushed them off and not come back for more. But he had the guts to laugh at her.

"Hey, it wasn't my fault your side lost the case. Your guy had money to hire the best expert witness, and that was you. But he shouldn't have tried to hack the Air Force and then find a bad hacker to cover his tracks. You didn't have a chance."

Then Major Young pulled out the other chair at her table, moved it closer to her and sat.

"Don't hate me. I was just doing my job," he said.

Jen didn't notice any hint of contrition in his voice. Arrogant dude. But then, she'd thought the same thing at the trial.

She refused to be intimidated by him and have her dinner ruined She sipped from her wine glass, twirled more fettuccine on her fork and chewed slowly as he watched silently. She took another small bite and still he watched without a word.

Jen put her fork down and glared at him, hoping her tactic worked and she didn't have to resort to calling over the maître d'.

Instead of removing himself or quailing under her glare, he laughed again. A deep, rich, way-too-enticing laugh, which would work on 99.9 percent of the female population. She, however, was the other 0.1 percent.

"Jennifer Malone, perhaps you do deserve your nickname, Madame Ice Queen." He shivered dramatically. "But frankly, that frozen attitude isn't working here, not for me anyway."

He grabbed the bottle of Merlot on the table, looked at the label, picked up her glass, gave it a sniff, and took a sip.

Jen couldn't help it—her eyes widened and a gasp escaped.

"Good choice. Nice whisper of black cherry."

Handing her back the glass, she automatically took a sip to see if he was right.

He was. And before she could wipe her mouth of the droplet she felt clinging to her lips, he wiped it away with his finger.

Then licked the droplet off said finger. "Was I right?"

"Yes."

His grin grew wider with a hint of wickedness that sent a quiver of erotic arrows deep into her body. Pushing back his chair, Major Brice Young winked at her, then walked out of the restaurant with an easy gait.

Damn him. On so many levels.

She wasn't on the losing end of many cases, her expert witness testimony was just that, expert. But somehow the evidence had been tampered with and the Major had found the exchange of data. Her client got slammed with an enormous fine and a PR nightmare. Government one, Jen zero, and she was a bad loser.

And how she hated that moniker, Madame Ice Queen. She wasn't. She had feelings, hot, cold, anger, love, and lust, like any other person. She just kept them tucked away. It was a defensive strategy for her business, and usually it worked quite well.

Jen picked up the wine glass and drank deeply, realizing as she did that her lips touched the same spot as his, and another arrow found its mark deep inside her.

Really? On Christmas Eve she was having a stab of lust for a man she despised? *You know, you really are a bad loser. Despise? That's a bit strong.*

Dislike?

Better.

Pushing away her plate of cooling pasta, Jen stared out of the enormous windows of the restaurant spanning the upper two floors of the hotel. Atop the distant Washington Monument, red beacons flashed in the freshly falling snow. She looked down to see that the Washington Mall was all but deserted and Jen realized she was homesick.

The frequent traveling was beginning to drag on her. With the anonymous hotels, meetings in concrete office buildings and countless courtrooms she visited all over the country, everything blurred together into a dreary shade of beige.

Refusing dessert, Jen signed her room number to the bill and headed down two floors to her suite.

After kicking off her black stilettos and yanking off her blouse and black pencil skirt, she pulled back the covers and lay on the soft white sheets, still wearing the scraps of lace that passed for her undies. Glancing at the time on her cell phone, she saw with a pang that it was past midnight on the east coast. Christmas Day at this end of the country.

Instead of being 1400 miles away, Jen should be back in Boulder, Colorado, celebrating Christmas Eve as usual with her best buddy, Annie Hamilton.

They'd be sitting in front of Annie's Christmas tree decorated with a gazillion lights, with her eclectic, treasured ornaments bending every bough.

Annie would have lit the fire, its flames creating tranquility as they reflected off the crushed glass beneath them.

And instead of hotel fare, they'd be noshing on Annie's famous homemade fettuccine Alfredo, wine glasses close at hand, and the bottle within easy reach.

What was her best bud doing right now? Was she with Cole, her new next-door neighbor, and his boys? Jen had met Cole, and Annie couldn't have fallen for a better guy. Now if she'd just realize he was the *right* guy.

"Merry Christmas, Annie. I hope it's perfect for you. Sweet dreams," she whispered into the ether.

Jen knew she should get some sleep before this

mysterious meeting tomorrow, but whether she closed or eyes or stared at the ceiling, the image of Major Brice Young's face played in front of her.

Dark gray eyes with flecks of gold, almost eerie in their color. Lips that sucked that droplet of wine. A chin that said Brice brooked no resistance. And what was with the long hair that curled at the nape of his neck, in stark contrast with his crisp white shirt? Not military hair for sure.

Madame Ice Queen.

Jen closed her eyes against the burn of tears, refusing to let a single one fall as she replayed the sting in Brice's voice. She was strong, independent, and she wasn't an Ice Queen. She wasn't.

Once again, she wished she were home.

Damn, but Jennifer Malone was a frozen woman, albeit a stunning "Madame Ice Queen."

Brice had approached her with the intent of giving her a head's up about tomorrow's meeting and how important it was for him to have her there. Knowing she wouldn't be keen about being around him at all, he planned all his arguments to win her over.

Then, after her first rebuff in the bar, his contrary streak challenged him to find out if she had a heart that pumped blood and not ice water under that white blouse.

And now, freezing in the parking lot of the hotel, scraping the ice off his car, he smiled grimly. Glacial water ran through her veins, and she was just going to have to find out the punch line of tomorrow's meeting, at the meeting.

Wounded ego, eh, man?

Perhaps, but there was no denying the flood of plain old desire that had surged through him as he'd followed his knee-jerk impulse to wipe that droplet off her lip.

He shouldn't have done it. Plain and simple.

Yet, for a brief second, he thought he saw fire in her gaze. And that enticed him. If he could only figure out how to make it happen again.

Man, you've got enough on your plate without adding skirt chasing. Besides, you're still singed from Bethany.

All true, he acknowledged to his inner voice. One he should listen to more often. It had warned him about his ex-wife, but he'd been too deafened by the attention she lavished on him and, heck, the hot sex, to hear a word of it.

Anyway, this project was too important and time too short to do anything other than work.

Too bad for Miss Jennifer Malone, who could use the thawing.

Brice entered his small, and supposedly temporary apartment, though he'd been living here a year. Not bothering to flip on the lights, he dodged his cheap futon couch and laminated coffee table. With a few strides he crossed to the sliding glass door fronting his pitifully small balcony.

He watched the white crystals drift down, piling on the deck's railing, and hoped the flimsy thing would hold up under the snow's weight.

And damn, in his haste to get to the hotel's restaurant, he'd forgotten to turn up the heat. Drafts of cold air puffed through the ancient window's seals. Brice pulled his wool scarf tight and kept on his overcoat while he stared at the bleakness and beauty of the scene in front of him.

Had he made the right choice retiring from the military? The money from this new venture could be astronomical, and he'd get his retirement pay on top of that. He could work his own hours. Especially now that Bethany was out of the picture, always demanding that her social and shopping needs be met during his off-duty time.

One separation painful, the other not.

His marriage had been short-lived, and all he felt now was relief.

But his time in the Air Force was more than his job—it had been his life, and that seemed played out as well.

All in all, both splits seemed right, or in the case of Bethany, more than right. Resuming bachelorhood hadn't been all that hard if you didn't count the accommodations.

Being a civvie? Well, that was going to be damn hard.

Finally, he turned from the window and headed into his bedroom. A sleeper compartment on a train had more space. It didn't take him long to pack his bag, he wasn't going to be gone more than a week. Then stripping quickly, he pulled on clean but well-worn sweats. He set the alarm, knowing he'd get the evil eye from the General if he was late to the meeting tomorrow. And finally slipped into his cold bed.

Then he couldn't get that one fiery flash from Jennifer

Malone out of his brain. Beautiful and smart. *Don't forget tough as nails.*

Well, he was used to tough. Just wait, there were going to be some sparks that had nothing to do with physical attraction. This project was too important to blow and he would brook no interference.

Brice smiled as sleep began to claim him.

JEN FOLLOWED HER ESCORT THROUGH THE UTILITARIAN corridors of the Pentagon, swearing she'd never again work on Christmas Day.

She paused outside the meeting room door to straighten her black sweater and smooth her black slim skirt. Wrapping the red scarf around her neck a bit tighter, she glanced down her black tight-clad legs and smiled at her other spot of bright holiday color, her red shorty boots. It was Christmas, and if she wanted to wear red, then fine.

The officer who'd escorted her flashed her a smile. "Love the boots," she said. "Ready?"

"Ready. And thanks, they were a whim, but I love 'em too."

The officer opened the door.

Her overcoat folded over one arm and laptop case in her other hand, Jen entered the room, confidence beaming from every pore. As usual for the Pentagon, she found a room full of men in uniform.

And thankfully, there wasn't a single Major Brice Young in the group.

When the Pentagon asked her to be *the* beta tester of a new system their brightest cyber geek had just finished, she was intrigued.

And when the general named a figure and, in the same breath, asked if she could be here in a day, she was hooked. You just didn't turn down a job like this, and anyway, she liked working in tandem with the brains in the military. They didn't often come onto her, and stars on any shoulders didn't faze her.

Nor did being the only woman in the room. Well, it honestly bothered her that there weren't other women included in the ranks of the men before her, but not being the only female in the room.

"Gentlemen," she said as they moved forward almost as a unit. *Ah, military precision.*

After shaking hands, she took her seat, opened her laptop. Then waited.

The men were still standing. She counted, added herself and realized there was one extra chair.

"Sorry, sir. Snarl on the 110."

Jen closed her eyes. No bloody way could this happen. *Damn and double damn.*

"And Ms. Malone, glad to see you made it here safely."

Jen nodded, settling her face into a serene expression. 'I had a driver, courtesy of General Cartwright."

Everyone sat. The general cleared his throat and drew all eyes, except hers.

She snuck a peek at Brice, only to see his grin while his eyes remained front and center.

And he didn't have on a uniform. What was going on?

"We want Vader to be on line in the next ten days," the General said.

Vader? She'd heard of this Vader. The name was the scuttlebutt in the industry, but no one knew anything about it.

"And the testing is to be done by you, Ms. Malone. Mr. Young is going to throw everything he can at the system. We want to know if Vader can block cyber attacks and track who is responsible for said attacks."

She was going to get to test Vader?

Jen would have done it for free just to see how it worked. *Merry Christmas to me.*

Now she looked directly at Brice only to see that his grin, while still there, had a weary look to it. Nor was she wrong last night. He did have dark smudges under his eyes. "Mr. Young? What happened to Major Young?" she blurted out.

"Retired after my twenty."

"Yes, damn him," General Cartwright added. "Dangling the rank of Lieutenant Colonel wasn't enough to keep him in longer."

She'd thought Brice would have been a general some day. He had the attitude when he presented his evidence at the trial. Tearing apart the one bit of cyber evidence that she and her employee, Todd Sargent, had been leery about.

Todd hated the major with a passion and despised losing as much as she did. "I'm guessing you and I are going to be working together testing Vader?" she asked Brice.

He nodded, and his grin grew wider.

"Why you?" Vader or not, why did this particular man have to be the one she was to be partnered with?

"Vader is my baby, and I need to watch it grow up."

He designed Vader? Holy moly. This guy must be brilliant.

Suddenly, she felt as if she were back in the "slow group" during elementary school. She wasn't stupid, hadn't been then, but she had been bored. To tears. She'd hated school until Doc Hamilton suggested the principal move her into his daughter, Annie's, class, a grade ahead. Then she began to excel, proving her surrogate father was dead right.

She shook off the memory. It needed to be erased, but somehow it always cropped up when she was being tested. She reminded herself that she was as smart as Brice Young, and she'd prove it to him.

"I test in *my* lab," she said, making the snap decision while keeping her voice flat to cover her excitement over this new challenge. She needed to be on her turf to make sure she had all *her* tools right at her fingertips.

"That's fine. I like Colorado."

"Are you bringing along a ton of equipment?"

"Nope. Laptop, tablet, Vader, some clothes and me. Vader isn't small, but it's portable."

"Good. I assume we'll connect it to the public Internet?"

"Yup, I've got some very interesting attack scenarios, and you're going to tell me what gets through and how."

"Maybe even why."

"You're that good?"

"Isn't that why you wanted me?" Jen asked with a sudden spurt of confidence.

"So, I gather we're set, Ms. Malone?" the general asked.

"Yes, sir."

"Good, then let's get started. Clock's ticking. I'll call Andrews and tell them that you're on your way, while you pick up your gear at the hotel. You'll head home courtesy of the Air Force."

Brice started to salute, then stuck out his hand to General Cartwright, who clasped it warmly. It was obvious to Jen the two were close and, she'd guess, could now afford to show it. They stood by the door, waiting for her.

Jen shook the general's hand. "It'll be a pleasure to test Vader, General. Thank you for allowing me this fun."

"Not my idea, though I liked it. It was his." The general nodded to Major Brice Young, retired.

2

——————

"GOT A SNOW BRUSH?" BRICE ASKED AFTER THE COURTESY van stopped in front of Jen's X5 at the parking lot on the outskirts of Denver International Airport. They were the only passengers, and the driver was nice enough to wait a few minutes while Brice cleaned off the tailgate so he could get Vader tucked into the SUV.

It surprised Brice that Jen didn't have a limo come and drive her home, and if she drove, why not park in the covered parking building? A woman of her means could afford to do either.

"Of course I have a snow brush, and I can handle it."

"I'm sure you can, but why don't you start the car and warm it up. I'll brush and we can get Vader into the car and then the driver of the van can leave. Teamwork, you know, and we can start practicing now."

Her narrowed eyes didn't faze him, and he cheerfully went to work after she handed him the brush. He cleaned the tailgate and Jen pushed a button for it to lift. He secured Vader and then tipped the driver handsomely for his patience.

Finally, after a last brush over the silver metallic surface of the BMW and a final sweep over his clothes to remove the snow that had cascaded off the car and onto him, Brice climbed into the warming vehicle. It didn't matter that his loafers were filled with snow or that he'd brought totally the wrong shoes and his feet were freezing. It mattered that he helped, and a little prod about teamwork didn't hurt.

"Do you have a hotel reservation?" she asked, putting the BMW in reverse and backing out of the tight space.

"Nope. Nothing was available in town. I figured you've gotta have an extra room at your place. So I thought I'd bunk there."

She slammed on the brakes. "You thought wrong."

"I don't think so. We're going to be working hard on Vader. I'm going to throw everything I've got at this and time is short. Shorter than I planned."

He sat back and let Jen drive undisturbed. Sort of. She was gripping the steering wheel pretty tightly.

The falling snow was perfect for Christmas day, and what little light remained was fading as dusk fell early in winter. The headlights illuminated the torrent of flakes as they accelerated through them, creating a near whiteout. But the BMW was cozy, warm and excellent in the snow. The added plus was Jen's driving skill.

They'd gained two hours going west but lost time when they'd stopped by the DC hotel for her to pack. Then they'd had to fight the Christmas day traffic out to Andrews. Combined with clearance delays and a couple of last-minute VIP passengers, they weren't wheels-up until nearly 3 p.m.

However, the jet was small and fast, and the trip was quicker than flying commercial. He worked the whole time, and Jen was buried in her computer as well.

Brice leaned his head against the SUV's leather headrest. He'd admit, if only to himself, that he was dog tired. The day, heck the last three months, had been stressful. It was show time for his baby.

He realized that he'd stupidly antagonized Jen yesterday. First by bringing up her missed appearance at the convention, knowing she'd been obligated to the job first and foremost. And second, that overt sexual move of stealing that droplet of wine from her lips. *That* whole bit was spontaneous.

Yes, he knew she was going to be at the hotel, and he'd planned to soften her up before their official meeting today. He needed her to help with Vader, so why had he behaved so rashly? Maybe it was the way the white silk blouse had draped across her breasts, coupled with the tight skirt. She looked prim and proper with the stark colors, and deliciously sexy with the clothes.

He glanced at her as she concentrated on the road, her face lit by the few oncoming cars. *Maybe it was because she was a stunning woman who wore a facade of iciness that begged to be melted.*

His phone buzzed loudly. He glanced at the number

and couldn't hold back his sigh. "Excuse me while I take this."

Before he could say hello, he was holding the phone away from his ear, knowing Jen could hear everything. Dammit.

"Bethany, stop yelling."

"When are you taking your stupid piano out. I've had it here for a year and you said a couple of months. It was in the way for my Christmas party last night, and I'm tired of dealing with it."

"I'm hoping nobody spilled a drink on it."

"It would serve you right if someone did, but no, it's clean and dry. I'm warning you—"

"I'll have it moved when I get home." *Home?* His apartment wasn't home and there wasn't room for a decent couch, let alone a grand piano. He needed to buy a house or condo and set down some roots. And after Vader was put into service, he'd seriously think about where that might be.

"I can't hear you. This connection is really scratchy. Where are you?"

She probably thought the poor cell phone reception was something he was manipulating on purpose—he certainly had the skills.

"Colorado, working on Vader. It's snowing, which is probably why the connection is bad."

"Vader. You screwed me in that deal on purpose."

You got that one right.

"Bethany, we're done, it's over. Been over for a long time."

Like from the start.

Brice pushed the disconnect button and turned to Jen. "Sorry you had to hear any of that." He stuffed the phone into his pocket but really wanted to throw it out the window. Why had he married Bethany?

Because she thought you were a god in uniform, and you liked that, a lot.

They'd met at Hanger One, the officer's lounge at The Club at Andrews AFB. They'd both come with other people but left with each other, something Brice had never done in his life. That was his first regret in a series of regretful moments. He realized he never loved Bethany, in fact never even really liked her.

Being an object of appeal was a powerful blinder to truth.

Afterwards, he realized that she wanted him for the uniform—and the rank—assuming he'd climb all the way to general. By the time comprehension hit his pea brain, it was too late.

"You okay?"

"Yes. You probably guessed, but that was my ex-wife."

"Hmmm. Sorry you felt you had to divorce."

Oddly, Jen sounded a bit prim and judgmental, even old fashioned. "Thanks, I'm not."

"How long were you married?"

"A bit less than a year. Divorced for about the same amount of time."

"Wow, and you gave her everything but the piano?"

"Yep, she doesn't get my pension. She got the car, which is less than new, the house with its large mortgage, and what's inside it—except the piano—which isn't much. But it's in a great neighborhood. I'm betting she'll sell it. Basically she thought she was going to get a general in another fifteen years or so, and I didn't want to be one."

"Generous of you for less than a year of wedded bliss."

Brice met her glance, about to protest, until he saw a glimmer of jesting in her eyes, telling him the absurdness of his situation wasn't lost on her.

Well, well, well. Maybe, if he was lucky, Jennifer Malone had a funny bone tucked inside that long, lean body.

He snorted. "I'm glad to be done with her. It was a mistake all the way around."

Her smile vanished instantly. What did he say?

"Back to *our* living arrangements."

"Jennifer, I know you have two labs; the one where you meet clients and where your employees work is located in downtown Boulder. And then there's your private lab, adjacent to your house. I can sleep in the private lab, assuming you have something horizontal for me to sleep on. You get your house. Better?"

"Gee, thanks," she said in a perfectly droll voice. "And the floor is horizontal."

Laughter erupted. He couldn't help it. This woman was quick and she was funny. Why was she such a cold bird the rest of the time?

"Just need a blanket and a pillow." His stomach rumbled. "Can we call for take-out and start work?"

"Christmas, remember?"

"Yeah, sorry. We can start tomorrow."

"No, I didn't mean that. Take-out other than pizza might be impossible, especially with this snow. Actually I can cook, I just don't do it often. My friend Annie is a whiz, so when I'm in town I mooch a meal at her place. How about an omelet and all the trimmings?"

"Like bacon?" he asked hopefully.

"And fresh bread loaded with real butter that when I broil turns brown and bubbly on top."

Brice wiped his mouth, afraid he really was drooling. "You're on. And please tell me that there is a horizontal surface in your lab other than the floor?"

"Sure, the desk."

Brice grinned again.

Jen turned into a long cobble driveway, pushed a button, and the garage door opened. Wow, a three-car garage and a house that looked big enough for two families.

Surely there was an extra bedroom in the place.

She pulled the BMW into the garage, empty of clutter except for garbage and recycle containers neatly arranged in a row, and turned off the ignition.

They were here. He wondered just which person she was going to be to work with. He'd wanted the best, with credentials everyone would instantly recognize. Would she be the Ice Queen, or this other Jennifer Malone, a witty and sexy woman with a brain he was envious of?

JEN HELD OPEN THE CONNECTING DOOR FROM THE GARAGE into her kitchen. Brice set his precious cargo on the small rug near the back door and then headed back to get the rest of their gear.

She stared at the shiny graphite, specially-designed case, guessing it held a super-fast, high-end computer loaded with the software Brice designed. Jen was anxious to see what Vader would do to protect and isolate cyber threats, from simple denial-of-service aimed at websites and online stores to foreign cyber terrorism.

Tomorrow would tell.

Moving into her great room, Jen debated turning on the lights gracing the small Christmas tree. It didn't feel like Christmas. Then in a rush, she flipped the switch. *Annie would be ashamed of you. It's Christmas day for goodness sakes.*

Jen felt Brice behind her and wondered what he thought about her sad ode to the season.

"I didn't even put one up," he said. "Even so, that is the Charlie Browny-ist Christmas Tree I've ever seen in real life."

"I know, it's sad. It needs some magic. Annie does Christmas like no other person in the world. Not only do I mooch dinner from her, I mooch Christmas as well. I just never know if I'm going to be here or not, so I rarely bother to decorate much."

She heard the wistfulness in her voice, letting a chink in her armor show. But it was hard to be tough right now. After all, as she'd just reminded herself, it was Christmas day with snow falling, everything looking picture-postcard perfect outside.

And she was alone.

Maybe not technically alone, but certainly without a person to call honey, darling or even babe.

"It looks like Santa visited though." Brice pointed to a couple of wrapped packages on the table next to the tree.

Jen sucked it up and pushed the pity away. "I always trust in Santa. *He* hasn't failed me yet."

God, another chink just revealed. Maybe Brice didn't get that one. However a quick glance at him as she finished turning on the living room lights proved her wrong. He had a brow raised in question.

Jen sure as hell wasn't going into her lack of love life with him. "Would you mind lighting the fire while I start the bacon?" she asked, sidestepping her unintended reveal.

"Sure, but I don't see any logs."

"Ah, a trick I got from Annie." Jen handed him the remote for the fireplace and let him figure it out.

Stepping into her kitchen gave her a moment alone, a second to catch her breath and steady herself. She and Brice hadn't been apart since this morning unless you counted using the jet's facilities, and she was surrounded by his presence. Then there was the subtle connection she'd felt since they'd left the Pentagon.

A sense of fitting with someone.

A feeling she didn't want or trust. *Liar, you'd love to have a relationship that was equal, witty, fun.*

Pushing that fruitless thought aside, she turned to the

fridge and pulled out bacon, eggs, veggies, cheese and bread.

Jen hadn't been kidding when she said she liked to cook. It was something she learned from Annie, who was by far the better cook. But Jen knew if she did it more often, they would be neck and neck in any cooking competition.

She stopped turning the bacon as she realized she used the word *competition*. Why did she think everything had to be a test of who was better?

"I hope you're letting that cool enough for me to nibble on?"

She blinked at Brice's pleading voice and realized she still held the bacon midair in her tongs. "Sorry, it's not quite done. Another few minutes. Did you want to get your bag unpacked?"

"Sure, show me the room."

Jen pointed to the small building at the edge of her yard.

"Ah, your lab."

"Yep."

"You're really going to make me sleep in your lab?"

"Sure. You'll feel right at home."

Turning the heat down so the bacon wouldn't burn, Jen moved to the back door and turned on the yard lights, illuminating the pathway, covered by a good foot of snow. "You'll have to walk through the white stuff, but you'll be okay once you get a path going."

"I need boots."

She looked down to see his shoes. "Seriously, you wore

loafers to Colorado in winter?" Jen almost caved and told him about the guest suite in the house, but decided at least for tonight to give tit for tat. No reservations, then deal with it.

And she had this sneaking sense that Brice thought if he smiled hard enough, she'd cave. No way, this was business. She knew too much about him already. He was gorgeous, but he was divorced.

"Hey, there's nothing wrong with loafers, you guys plow sidewalks in Colorado right?"

"Right. Public sidewalks."

And he was funny.

Keeping her face straight was an effort, but she won the battle as Brice's shoulders slumped. He trudged out of the kitchen as she bit down her smile, returning moments later, suitcase and laptop in hand.

"Bacon will be ready by the time you unpack."

Stepping out into the snowy night, he looked back at her with big, sad, puppy-dog eyes.

Oh, mean trick.

Instead of giving in, she waved cheerfully, and Brice turned back to carving a path through the snow to the lab.

Guilt bit her and she turned on the walkway heating system. The bluestone-paved path, which ran from her house to the lab, had tubing beneath it that pumped heated antifreeze through the lines. A neat solution she'd had installed when years ago at 2 in the morning—after tossing, turning and punching her pillow—Jen finally figured out the solution to a complex problem that had plagued her for a week.

Not wanting to risk waiting until the morning to try out her idea, she ran across the snowy yard, slipped, and fell on her bum. It didn't hurt, but snow filled her sweatpants and fell down her shirt.

The next day she made a call to her landscapers and had the heating system on order.

Annie hadn't understood why Jen didn't want the lab in her house. After all, Annie often burned the midnight oil, and her office was right across the hall from her bedroom. But after Jen had explained that either Todd or Susan, her two employees, might need to come to her private lab to work on a problem or check a solution, Annie got it.

So she'd built the lab in what was originally going to be the pool house. She sure as hell didn't have time to care for or even use a pool. At least not at this point in her life.

The back door opened, letting in a blast of frigid air as Brice walked in. Perfect. The last of the bacon was just finished cooking.

He took off his shoes, and she laughed when she realized he'd put plastic bags over them for protection. "Did you find everything?"

"Yeah, cozy set up, even a couch, which I can barely fit on."

She smiled at his beseeching expression and sized up his six-foot-plus frame. "Nice try. It pulls out into a bed. Why buy a simple couch when you can get a bed as well?"

"If it's anything like the bed in the apartment I'm renting, I'll sleep on the floor."

"It's very comfortable, so no worries." She put the

bacon onto a paper-towel-lined platter and held it out to Brice. "Careful, it's hot."

He ate one piece quickly and reached for another. "This is really good, where'd you buy it?"

"Maine."

His eyebrows rose. "No, really."

"Yes, really. It's one of my splurges and reminds me of home. I order a few pounds every couple of months from a small farm outside the town I grew up in. I keep some in the freezer."

"And your eggs, where do they come from?"

Again, unbidden laughter rolled up from her belly. She had to be careful—this man had made her laugh more in a few hours than several of her more recent dates did during their entire time together. "There's this awesome place called a market, King Soopers, to be exact."

"Hmmm, I've heard of those kinds of stores, but they scare me."

"You're what, at least thirty-eight, and a grocery store scares you?"

"Forty, and yes, they do."

"How are you at chopping up peppers?"

"Which end of the knife do I use?" he said with a grin. "But I can learn, if you'll teach me."

Teach him? Standing body next to body while she showed him how to curl his fingers under on top of the food and make the proper undulating movement with the knife?

"Maybe later."

"Shucks."

"Seriously?" She looked at him, mouth open. "Shucks?"

"Sure, it's a perfectly good word."

"For a boy from Kansas," Jen said in a lighthearted tone.

"Found me out."

"Seriously?"

"There *are* other words in the dictionary. Yes, I grew up on a farm in Kansas. And I only use shucks when I'm trying to get into a lady's good graces."

"Huh, that's an interesting technique. Okay, no knives for you. How are you with a bottle opener?"

"Expert, gold medaled in the sport. Point out the bottle."

"It's in the fridge, the pinot grigio, if that's okay with you?" She handed him the opener.

He nodded and looked around, then headed in the right direction toward the refrigerator, covered in wood that matched her cabinets.

"Pretty fancy gear you got in here."

Jen shrugged as she put the peppers, onions and mushrooms into the skillet with the browning butter. Immediately the air filled with one of her favorite aromas and her stomach rumbled.

A huge growl came straight from Brice's belly. "That smells heavenly. I'm starved."

"I can tell." She kept one eye on the veggies as they sautéed and the other on Brice as he expertly removed the cork, found the right wine glasses in her cabinet and poured.

"Seriously," he drew the word out with a wicked grin. "This kitchen is like a pro's outfit."

She looked around with pride. Loving modern, the cabinets were bamboo and sleek, with stainless steel handles. The travertine countertops weren't the most practical; they needed sealing every year, but she didn't mind, because they were perfect. Her stove was a six-burner pro stainless steel workhorse and she had two sinks, just in case she had someone to cook with. A wish that wasn't often fulfilled.

Didn't look like Brice was going to fulfill it either.

In couple of minutes the eggs were set, the veggies spooned in, cheese sprinkled on top and the omelet flipped.

Jen put the bread under the broiler and watched it carefully as it turned brown and the butter bubbled. Another one of her favorite cooking scents.

"Grab some silverware, and we're about ready."

Brice followed her to the dining table in the area she'd created in her open living space dedicated to eating.

She waited for Brice's verdict on the omelet, wondering why it mattered so much.

He didn't pick up his fork.

Quirking a brow, she got a smile in return.

"Ladies first."

"Guests first."

Not needing a second urging, Brice dug in. He ate steadily until half his omelet was gone. "Shucks, you're a mighty fine cook."

"You keep up that hayseed attitude, and it's the last meal you're getting."

Which earned the grin she was hoping for. Brice Young was quite the contradiction. Too bad he was divorced.

Why? You never mix business with pleasure anyway.

Maybe I would this time.

3

"Brrr, it'd cold out there. Coffee smells good, and what's cooking? I could smell the cinnamon across the yard." Brice walked into Jen's kitchen, ready for the first cup of the day and the challenge of the next week. It was going to be stimulating in so many ways.

He'd pulled on jeans and his ancient Air Force Academy sweatshirt...just to remind her who she was dealing with.

The kitchen was empty, but a lone mug sat on the counter. He quickly figured which of the fancy coffee machine's buttons to push. Within seconds, the beans were grinding and then a hissing shot of steam followed by rich brew filling his cup. He was in heaven from the dark scent of the coffee, and he hadn't even had a taste.

Once made, he sipped it straight as it came out of the machine, black, and wondered where Jen was. Dare he wander the house?

"Oh, you're up," Jen said as she strode into the kitchen.

"I've got vanilla and cinnamon French toast warming in the oven, and some bacon left from last night. Maybe one or two pieces," she finished with a smile.

And damn if a rock didn't plummet in his stomach. Brice didn't trust his instincts around women after his mistake with Bethany. However, Jennifer was bright, funny when she let herself be, and even when she was being droll or sarcastic, she delivered good zingers. He was drawn to this side of her. And he was surprised she hadn't yet donned her Madame Ice Queen persona today.

"I change the minute we go to work," she said.

He stared at her steadily over the rim of his cup. Spooky that she'd read his mind. "Okay, in that case, we'll wait to plan strategy until after we eat."

Breakfast was devoured quickly, four thick slices of French toast for him and two for Jen, who graciously gave him the bacon. All *three* slices. And then he did the dishes as he'd done last night. Fair was fair.

"Ready to begin?" he said, moving toward the back door.

"Yep. Where are you headed?"

"To your lab."

"Ah, no. We're going to my office."

That took him aback. He was sure they were going to work in the small and intimate confines of her home lab. He'd even made the bed and cleaned up the bathroom so it didn't look like he'd taken over the space.

"Well then, let me grab my gear, load Vader into the BMW, and we're off."

Jen drove the snow-packed neighborhood street

expertly, and when they turned onto the major street, identified as Broadway on the sign, and started down the steep hill, the city of Boulder spread out below him.

"God, now that is a beautiful sight. How do you ever leave this place?"

"Business calls. I can't do it all from here."

He shook his head. "Man, I'd try." The city, with its coat of fresh snow, lay nestled at the base of the red sandstone of the flatirons jutting up against the mountains, both blanketed with more of the white stuff.

Brice recalled the intense blue of the Colorado sky from his Academy days in Colorado Springs, and the memory brought a tinge of nostalgia for those days twenty plus years ago. Boulder was more than picture postcard pretty, it felt like a place where he could set down roots.

While at the Academy, he'd been to the city once or twice, but it was for pre-season football games at the University, and he hadn't wandered much off the campus unless it was to a bar on the Pearl Street Mall. But this, this was amazing, something he could wake up to winter or summer.

"Can you see all this from your house?"

Jen looked at him with surprise. "Sure, in fact you could see it as you walked from the lab to the house this morning."

"I was focused on which scenario to throw at you first, thinking we'd be working at home, so didn't pay attention."

"I thought it would be wiser to work at the office," she said, with a tiny bit of Madame Ice Queen in her voice.

"Why? Afraid of me?" he teased.

She braked for a light and turned to look at him. He took the opportunity to waggle his brows.

Which achieved his purpose.

Jen cracked a smile. "Work, remember? We're short-term colleagues, and I never mix business with pleasure."

Her words totally undermined his objective. Still, it was fun to bait her. "You are far too serious, you know."

"So I've been told. But that's why you chose me to see if Vader will work as promised."

Touché.

Pulling into a parking building, she aimed for one of the six *Reserved for* ForceOne spots. She took the first one, so he guessed neither of her employees was at work yet.

Good. It would be easier to work on breaking her frozen work attitude if she didn't have employees around to witness it.

"Why six spots if there are three of you at ForceOne?" he asked.

"Clients need to park, too."

Ah, good point to remember when he was setting up his office.

She'd loaned him a small cart she kept in the garage at the house so he could move Vader more easily from the parking garage to her office.

He pushed it through the snow as they walked diagonally from the parking building and across a narrow alley. Jen used a key card to get into the alley side door. Then she surprised him as they continued on through the minuscule foyer and exited onto the Pearl Street Mall.

Crews were busy shoveling the walks, while store

clerks hung After Christmas SALE signs in the windows. Couples walked arm in arm, and he itched to grab Jen's just to see what she would do.

"I love that old building when it's covered in fresh snow. It makes me feel as if I've gone back in time, all signs of our modern era erased. So forgive me that I'm keeping you and Vader in the cold for a minute more. In a couple of hours, it'll all have melted and we'll be back in the real world." She pointed to a building across the street. "That's our old courthouse, built around 1932. It's a—"

"Art Deco or Art Moderne style, isn't it? It's really cool."

"How did you know that? Oh wait, if you were at the Air Force Academy—you must have come to Boulder once in a while."

"Yeah, I did. But that's not why I know anything about the courthouse. Mom is an architect nut, studies it all the time. When we were kids and went anywhere, she told us all about every interesting building. Back then it got really boring, but as an adult I've found those lectures a great asset."

He was sure Jennifer wasn't aware of the longing her eyes held or that she bit one corner of her mouth as if to stop the flow of something. Then she nodded and shed all of that emotion.

"At night, this time of year, the courthouse is lit with green and red up-lights, and the fountain has arches of lights that look like frozen water."

"Night comes early in winter, so I guess I have a good chance of seeing it."

Jen smiled, but it felt less warm to him. In fact from the

moment they got in her SUV to drive to her office, she'd been adding layers to her facade of Ice Queen. She'd warned him that would happen, but he'd hoped he could keep it bay for the rest of his stay. He was beginning to know the warm side of her and much preferred it.

They walked back through the double stained-glass and wood door, and now he took in the detail of the small foyer, complete with a cherry wood bench that took up half the room while they took up the other half.

Small, even nondescript. You wouldn't know that somewhere on a floor above was one of the top cyber forensic shops in the world.

Jen pushed the elevator's button. "Top floor, great view, and quiet."

The elevator stopped, the doors slid open, and Brice noticed there was only one door on the floor. A small granite plate by the door was engraved with *ForceOne*. There was a key pad under a small metal cover which Jen swung up to reveal an electronic keypad lock. He recognized the design, knowing it would show the time and person who accessed the office. Good call if there was ever a chain of custody issue. A lock audit could be pulled.

Giving her privacy while she entered her code, he looked around. There were two cameras set in the ceiling, not obvious, but then he knew how to look for less-than-obvious anythings.

She opened the door and he was blown away by the space, letting loose a whistle, getting a smile from Jen in return.

On the left wall was a glass office he guessed would be Jen's.

A fourteen-foot marble table designed with a wood insert down the middle for power cord and data ports dominated the middle of the room. And damn if she didn't have eight of the chairs he coveted—Aerons—tucked around that massive table.

Against the windows were three work stations, giving each person a lot of space.

These were not run of the mill steel-and-laminate-top units, they were brushed stainless with mahogany tops. Each station had a built-in, digitally locked, evidence cabinet. There was a Mac Pro on each station, and he assumed a MacBook Pro in each cupboard.

And each station was neat. Unbelievable.

Ninety-nine percent of the labs he'd ever been in looked like a bomb went off, strewn with cables and hardware.

Additionally there was a big screen monitor on the wall for presentations and group problem solving, a coffee machine like the one she had at home and a fridge. He could live in this lab.

"Nice, very nice. Where is your server room?"

Jen moved to a door that also had a digital lock on it. She worked her numbers on the lock and pulled open the door.

"And do you have a bigger evidence locker?"

"Of course." Jen pointed to another door just outside her office. It looked plain, but it also had a keypad, and when he touched the surface, he realized it was a well disguised steel door.

Brice was impressed with ForceOne, the best lab he'd seen yet.

"When you're ready, we'll get Vader mounted in the server room. Let me get my computer booted up." She headed toward the work station closest to the corner.

"Don't you work in your office space?" Brice asked and nodded toward the glass office.

"No, when I do my own forensic work, I like to be around Todd or Susan. There's a synergy between us. And sometimes, as you know, it takes all of us to work a case. I only work in the office for meetings that need to be discreet or on the actual biz end, like bills and all that good stuff. Which I hate, by the way. Thankfully I have good accountants." Again she smiled.

And her smile, even less than one hundred percent of the available wattage, was truly irresistible. He could do nothing but smile back.

Then it became all business as she booted up her computer, pulled out her laptop from the side locker and set to work.

All of a sudden his palms were sweaty and his heart thrummed. This was it, Vader had been tested and retested, but by him. He knew the ins and outs and of course could have unintentionally made it easy for his baby to do its work. Now the attacks were for real.

He got Vader installed in the server room, then pulled out the chair at the neighboring workstation and sat, his legs suddenly rubbery. He turned on his laptop and pulled up his digital checklist.

"Okay, number one on the list, sign the pen letter, please." He wasn't stupid or naive, and by having Jen sign the penetration test authorization letter, allowing him to do the assault on her network and hold him harmless, he was also putting the first gold seal of approval on Vader. Nobody would sign such a legal document unless they were confident in the testing that was going to happen.

"I was going to ask you about that. Why not have me sign it back in DC?"

"Because once you agreed to do this, I knew you wouldn't back out, and I wanted to make it all happen in one spot at the moment of testing."

"You're really attached to your system—or maybe I should call it a beast—aren't you?"

He nodded and watched as she signed the agreement, feeling intense satisfaction as she finished and handed him back the document.

"Number two, Internet Service Provider notification. I don't want the police coming after me as a hacker attacking."

"Done."

They both swiveled to look at the door. Todd Sargent stood there, a plate of pastries in one hand, the other gripping the door knob.

Brice knew the man both from his reputation and personally from the trial where Jen and Todd had been the expert witnesses for the defense. Todd hadn't liked him then, and he was bristling with antagonism now.

Sore loser or not, this emotion was unwarranted and only made Brice want to figure out why. Maybe Jen and Todd were an item?

A small stone hit his stomach, yet in the same thought, Brice just couldn't see it. Jen wouldn't have a relationship with a co-worker.

Which counts you out as well.

JEN SHOULD HAVE FIGURED TODD WOULD SHOW UP AT THE lab, if for no other reason than to claim this was his territory. There were times when her employee was just too obsessive about things, but he was an amazing cyber forensics geek, so she tended to overlook his eccentricities. Anyway, she was used to them after six years, and the team of three worked well together.

She knew the minute she'd told Todd that Brice was the designer of Vader and she was beta testing it, Todd would be difficult about it.

Indeed he'd gone ballistic. Jen let him rant a bit via the emails she received while in flight to Colorado. Then, as his emails dwindled and stopped, she assumed he'd realized that the decision to take any cases or jobs for ForceOne was hers, solely.

Apparently not.

Brice stood and moved the short distance to the door. "Todd," he greeted, sticking out his hand, which her employee ignored.

But now she wondered if that was too wishful or naive

an assumption. Todd could be loyal to a fault, and until right now, it never seemed to be an issue other than an annoyance at times.

"Isn't Major Young the man who beat us this fall on the VidComNet case?" Todd directed his comment to her as if Brice wasn't in the room.

"One and the same," Brice said with a trace of amusement Jen picked up immediately. "And it's no longer major. I'm a free man."

Todd put down his platter of pastries, squarely in the middle of the conference table, pulled off the plastic wrap, and adjusted one of the four hand-made, chocolate-drenched éclairs nestled on the plate. Then stood back, apparently satisfied they were evenly spaced.

"Did you open my Christmas gift?" Todd asked her, abruptly changing the subject, as he was inclined to do.

"No, we didn't get back until late and started this early."

Todd simply nodded. His usual response. It was only when he was deep in work that he became animated.

"Besides, you know I never open gifts alone. I'm usually with Annie."

A pang of guilt hit her. She hadn't called her best friend last night to tell her she was home. And now she couldn't wait to tell her who she was home with.

Jen smiled with anticipation for their visit, sure Annie would have stories to tell her about Cole Evans, her dreamy next-door neighbor.

"Jennifer first," Todd said sharply.

Pulling herself back to the moment, she saw Brice's hand hovering over the platter.

"Of course, sorry. Ladies first."

Knowing Brice or Todd wouldn't take one until she did, she chose one of the four identical éclairs. "Brice, there are plates in the cupboard below the coffee machine, and napkins as well," she said.

He got them out and put them on the table in a pile.

Todd immediately folded the napkins, and put three in a row, with a plate above each. Jen finally couldn't wait and took a bite of the sinfully light pastry with real vanilla custard inside, topped by dark, deep chocolate flavored with orange.

She groaned with pleasure.

"Don't do that," Brice warned.

The gleam in his eyes almost elicited another groan. That was going to have to stop immediately, so she focused on Todd, who was now shooting daggers at Brice. "Thank you—"

"I know they're your favorites; it was no trouble making them. So when do we get to work?" Todd looked directly at her, then instantly switched his gaze to the table and moved Brice's coffee cup a bit to the left of his plate. She fully expected Brice to move it back, but his hands were busy with the pastry.

"Todd, there is no 'we' on this one. Just Jen and me."

Todd cocked his head and turned it to look at her. She'd always thought it a bird-like motion, but it came with the brilliance that was inside this man, so she accepted it as part of him. But now she wondered how it appeared to someone meeting Todd for the first time. Clients seemed to accept him, but was it only because of the reputation of her labs and her work?

"Jennifer and I work together here."

"Maybe on another gig, but not this one," Brice said easily, but with steel girding each word.

"Well, that will be a bit hard, as I have work to do here as well, unless you're closing the lab. Are you, Jennifer?"

"Of course not. Susan has case work as well. But this project is between Mr. Young and me," she said, hoping he got the message. If not, she was going to have to have a talk with Todd, something that wouldn't go well.

Todd blinked a couple of times and turned his focus to the remaining two pastries.

Jennifer couldn't see the differences between the pair, but he apparently could. Finally he chose, put his selection on his plate and moved to his station.

Where Brice had his laptop set up.

Damn, she should have told him not to set up there. But then she thought Todd was taking a few days off.

"Could you please..." she nodded to his gear and thankfully he got the hint.

"Conference table okay?"

"Perfect."

"Glad you like the éclairs, Jennifer. The orange is from my Satsuma tree," Todd said as he booted up his equipment. "And the chocolate's from Belgium."

~

WAS TODD GOING TO CHATTER CONSTANTLY? BRICE WAITED a minute to continue his checklist with Jennifer until the man booted up both his computers and seemed immediately engrossed in work.

"Okay, number three on my list, the rules of engagement," Brice said. "I will do everything I can to attack your network, but only the one you've set up for Vader to run behind."

"I'd expect nothing less if we're going to prove Vader is the beast you claim he is," Jen said.

The harder, clipped edge was back in her voice.

The mood in the lab had changed. Jen had fully switched into the mode he didn't like, and Brice had the oddest sensation that Todd was paying acute attention to them, even though he appeared to be buried in a project.

It was apparent that Brice was going to be considered the interloper here. Well, this was only going to last a week or less, and the vetting seal of approval Jen would give his system would go a long way to ease his suffering.

"I'll want the log files, and please note what Vader reports to you and when, so I can correlate the logs and the reports."

"Got it. I'm not a newbie at this."

"Just setting ground rules, so everything is reported fairly, and Vader flies through all this with an A plus." He heard the sharpness in his own voice.

Brice needed to focus on the task at hand. It was everything he'd worked to perfect during the last eighteen months, and he wasn't going to let some weird dude or frigid woman make him lose focus.

"Jennifer is nothing if not fair."

Brice simply nodded in agreement, not letting Todd get under his skin again. He sucked in a breath. "Okay, here goes." He found her network on the Internet without much difficulty, and began normal reconnaissance steps, scanning to find any vulnerabilities.

"Vader found you and blocked your computer after it saw your port-scanning attempts. The log shows all the information you'll need," Jen reported, voice neutral.

Just wait, he'd get her excited.

"Good, I'm starting slow to see just what he gives you for info," Brice said, not looking up from his computer, using keystroke after keystroke to launch attacks.

Vader wasn't just a tool the government could buy, it was as Jen called it, a beast that would change the level of protection anybody with seven hundred and fifty thousand to past a cool million could buy.

Vader would make him.

Finally he sat back in his chair, rolled his shoulders to get out some of the tension, and got up, intending to see if Jen needed another cup of coffee, because he certainly did.

As if Todd read his mind, he reached across their stations for her cup, refilled it and was back at his station all without a word or a glance in his direction.

No doubt about it, Brice was not part of the team.

He made his own coffee, moved to the windows and stared at the view below on the mall.

Even with the snow last night, the street was beginning to bustle with people bundled up against the cold. Then he spied a stray wearer of shorts, woolly socks, sandals, and a heavy sweater. Brice smiled, realizing some things didn't change. He'd seen the same thing when he'd been in Boulder all those years ago.

He was grateful for the height restrictions the city had enacted as he could see the mountains and the Flatirons from the window. No wonder Jen loved this office.

He turned to glance at her. Head bent with the overhead lighting reflecting off silky strands of golden blonde hair ... *knock it off. The challenge is her attitude, not fighting yourself over simple hormones.*

Brice wondered what Jen would have done for Christmas if she hadn't been in DC answering the call of Uncle Sam. She'd mentioned this friend Annie several times with deep fondness lacing her words. And Jen had said she often mooched Christmas off her buddy. But did Jen have any holiday traditions of her own? Like opening presents on Christmas Eve?

That one drove him nuts. Everyone knew Santa didn't come until Christmas day, so why ruin the joy of tearing into everything on that *one* day? Dad told him it was a Mom tradition, so he resigned himself to opening family presents on Christmas eve with Mom playing carols on the piano and Dad singing along in his deep baritone.

This year they were in California over the holidays to help Caroline's debut float in the Rose Parade.

He smiled, thinking of his diminutive sister guiding the building of a thirty-five-foot float that had to collapse to seventeen feet to go under the Sierra Madre Boulevard/I-210 freeway overpass. As well as directing over a hundred people in the placing of the flowers, seeds and bark. All for her two-year-old float-building company, *Always Young.*

She'd done several barges for San Antonio's River Walk flotilla and a couple of floats for the Orange bowl last year and Macy's parade this year. But she considered this the star in her crown.

While he waited for Jen and Vader to finish fending off this attack, he brought up Caro's website and looked at the progress of the build. Seeds had been added and flowers were now being cut, shredded or depetaled. And some were standing in funny little water vials, stuck in long trays, in a rainbow gradation of color.

The web cam she'd set up was hilarious to watch. It looked like total chaos, but he knew it was all carefully orchestrated by Caro. And there were his parents, working alongside their daughter. A longing he hadn't felt since his first few years in the service surged through him. He wanted to be with them, a family unit.

His attention was pulled from the web cam images by Jen as she swiveled her chair his direction, then stretched, pulling the black sweater up her ribcage, exposing skin.

He gulped.

Her low-slung jeans were snug, the sweater baggy, but the gap between was sleek, smooth flesh.

"The last logging was completed a few minutes ago, so I think we're done. I have to give you credit, Vader is pretty slick."

Whoa, he'd take that little crumb of praise. "Where were the sticking points?"

"Do you mind if we take a walk while talking? I need to move and my brain needs fresh air."

"Sure, it's only, what, ten degrees outside. Let's walk."

That worked. He got a grin from her, finally.

However, if they walked, then that meant he was going to leave Vader at ForceOne, alone with Todd. *For Godsakes, man, Jen wouldn't have hired anyone that wasn't A++ vetted.*

Todd would be fine with his beast. Even if the two men were on less than comfortable footing, he felt Todd wouldn't harm Jen or the company by sabotaging anything.

Next issue.

Brice hadn't packed boots. He'd figured Jen would request working at her lab, so when he'd packed the night before, for some reason, boots weren't on his mental checklist.

"Is there an outdoor store around here?"

Jen's laugh broke another huge chunk out of the barrier he'd felt go up a couple of hours ago, and some of the tense stiffness in his shoulders loosened.

"Maybe only a couple dozen in Boulder. What are you looking for? Warm shoes?"

"Yes, and a hat. I think I need to do some more exploring of Boulder before I head back to DC."

"I'd love to show you some of my favorite haunts."

He stopped in the middle of locking down his computer.

Damn if he wasn't going to get whiplash from the swift changes this woman made. "Okay, it's a deal."

"I need a break as well. I think I'll join you," Todd said,

right at Brice's shoulder. He nearly jumped. The man was a wraith.

Brice wracked his brain to find an excuse to be alone with Jen.

"Maybe later, Todd. Okay?" Jen said.

He nodded and that seemed to be the end of it. But when Brice looked back just before they walked out the lab's door, the wiry man wore a decidedly worried look.

What did he think Brice was going to do to Jen, kidnap her? Brainwash her?

Kiss her?

Now that was an idea.

After they left the office, he let Jen lead the way. West past the courthouse, across Broadway, and up a block to the end of the mall. Pine garland had been wrapped around each black metal lamppost along the outdoor pedestrian mall. Benches were plentiful, and the planters, though currently filled with snow, offered additional seating.

"I bet this place is always busy. It's really pleasant."

"You don't remember it?"

"Frankly, not much. It was usually night when we were here, and we weren't looking at the scenery, at least this scenery."

"Sorority girls?"

"Hey, we have women at the Academy as well. We looked at the females, they checked out the males."

That earned him an eye roll.

Jen stopped in front of an old-fashioned store near the

west end of the mall. "This is the Boulder Bookstore, where Annie signs a couple times a year."

"Then this Annie of yours is an author?"

"Yep, Annabelle Hamilton. She writes children's books. And in the spring, she has line of plush toys depicting some of her main characters. It's very exciting. I'd love for you to meet her while you're here. In fact, I'll ask her if she can make us dinner one night."

Jen's face softened and the glow of the deep bond she shared with Annie lit her eyes.

He wondered how Jen's eyes would look in the aftermath of a languorous love-making session.

She changed the subject, and he had to stop that interesting train of thought to focus on what she was telling him about Vader and where the sticky points were.

"So let's get back and I'll show you," she said, her voice ringing with anticipation.

They passed a Sushi restaurant and his stomach grumbled.

"How about lunch, then work?" he said.

Jen stopped abruptly by a bronze sculpture of a child on a swing and stared at him.

"What?"

"I'm going to have to add extra expenses to my bill for feeding you."

"General Cartwright can handle it."

"I don't know, you might break their budget."

He grinned, feeling more and more in tune with this woman.

"By the way, I meant to ask you, how did the military

get first dibs on your program. Isn't it going to be an open market product?"

"Yeah, but I gave Cartwright the chance to buy it first. National security and all that. Besides, and if you tell anyone this, I'll disavow it, Cartwright has been my mentor from the get-go, and I owe him big time."

"There's nothing wrong with having a mentor."

The wistfulness in her voice gave him pause.

4

"I gather you had a mentor?" Brice asked.

The racket from the crowds on the mall didn't stop Jen from hearing the gentleness in his voice. She realized it was far too easy to let down her defenses in front of him. What was it about him that made her want to confide? The only person she divulged any secrets to was Annie.

"Yes, I did. He's gone now. A wise man with great compassion."

Brice's mouth opened just as her cell phone rang. Holding up a finger, she took the call, knowing as she did so, it would annoy the man standing in front of her. And with luck, put them back on a less emotional plane.

"Annie! Belated Merry Christmas. Yes, I'm home, got here late last night. Starting work on beta testing a new system a developer has come up. Dinner tonight? Ummm... " She glanced at Brice, who nodded vigorously.

"Wait, back up, what did you just say? Cole will be there? And the boys?"

Brice was still nodding. The mention of boys didn't faze him.

"Yes, we'd love to come, and yes, we can celebrate tonight. I don't think Brice will mind. And," she drew out the word, "next year, I promise, Christmas here with you. See you at five-thirty. Want me to bring wine?"

Smiling, she disconnected the call. "Do you like sushi?" she asked Brice, who again nodded quickly. "How about shoe leather?" she joked to see if he would still nod.

"The way my stomach is rumbling, yes."

Jen punched in another number, "Hey, Todd, up for Hapa today? Is Susan there? Just you? Okay, we'll be back in a few."

Leading the way back up the street, they entered the long, narrow sushi restaurant. A black lacquer and wooden counter ran the distance to glass panels, with table seating against the opposite brick wall. Even on December twenty-sixth, the place was packed.

Jen placed her order, the usual along with two Mork and Mindy rolls, one for Todd and the other she'd share with Brice. After all, Mork and Mindy were Boulder celebs, making the Pearl Street Mall famous for a while.

"Miss Jennifer, you want delivered or wait? It's going to be awhile, even for you," he said with an apologetic bow.

Their host, Kazuo, dressed as always in tailored black slacks and a white shirt, open at the collar. Around his neck, an imperial green jade disk hung from a woven cord. Kazuo had once told her he'd worn it since birth, only taking it off to have it put on a larger cord. It was his family's tradition back in Kyoto.

"How about delivery then?" She pulled out her wallet, only to have Brice beat her as he handed over his card. About to protest, she caught the gleam of mischievousness in his eyes and bested him at this game by remaining silent, though it about killed her not to protest. She always paid her own way—it simply made life easier. Even on dates, if she initiated it, she paid. Simple.

On the return trip to the lab, one that should have only taken five minutes tops, Brice strolled, stopping at window displays, pointing out a massive geode, its cavity filled with rich amethyst crystals in one shop, and a black leather backpack with silver lightning bolts in another.

Jen was used to striding everywhere but had learned long ago when walking with petite Annie to shorten her gait. She expected Brice, who topped her own five-feet eight-inches by at least four more, to be a first-class strider. To get to the destination quickly. To her it wasn't the journey, but the destination, in everything she did. Later, when she retired, she'd slow down and appreciate the view.

"It really is the journey," Brice said mildly.

"Stop reading my mind."

"Why? You've read mine a couple of times. Fair is fair."

She grabbed his arm. "The sushi is going to get to the office before us." Which, as she expected might happen, quickened his pace.

Todd had the conference table cleaned off, the platter he'd brought this morning was sparkling clean, not a trace of éclair left, and napkins were laid out.

"I made the green tea."

"Sounds like this is a ForceOne ritual lunch," Brice said.

"I think Todd would have been a sushi chef if forensics hadn't grabbed hold of him first."

"There is a soothing rhythm to the cutting of the sashimi and the creating of rolls with precision that appeals," Todd said in a pleased voice.

Brice nodded. "I can see that."

Surprising Jen once again that he'd understood. "You have to use knives, Brice. Remember, you're knife challenged?"

"Which is exactly why I appreciate it all the more."

Jen felt Todd's glance and knew he had been excluded from their private joke and wasn't happy about it.

She'd never mixed pleasure and business before. Now it felt very much as if that line was smudging, even disappearing in spots. She needed to talk to Annie, to get back the perspective that had served her so well in the past.

Just then the door buzzer sounded, and this time Jen was prepared, with the tip folded and ready to go in her pocket as she let in their delivery.

Taking the boxes of sushi to Todd, she allowed him to lay them out in the order he preferred.

She watched Brice study her right-hand man as he opened the soy sauce packets and poured them into the little porcelain containers Kazuo knew Todd wanted and always included—which Todd later returned to the restaurant sparkling clean.

Then he stirred the wasabi into another tiny bowl and formed a perfect peak.

During all this, Brice's expression was priceless. Brow furrowed, then eyebrow raised as he rubbed his lower lip with his thumb.

Todd was odd, but a great detective who didn't mind the hours and had the patience needed to sort through files, bytes and bits.

Lunch went quickly, and while Todd cleaned up, something else he was particular about, she showed Brice just where Vader appeared to be too sensitive and didn't let some of the legitimate traffic through.

Brice made notes on his laptop and sent her the next attack. "Take your time, it's a bitch. We're going to jump around a bit, from simple attacks to more complicated. I don't want you or Vader to get complacent."

The minute she looked at the emerging logs, she knew this indeed was going to be tough. Brice was tunneling malicious traffic inside of legitimate traffic channels and Vader was inspecting everything instead of blocking all of it.

JEN SET TO WORK, MONITORING THE ATTACK AND VADER'S response. Brice worked his talents hard to create ruthless and relentless attacks. Imagining himself as the enemy, close to getting the passwords to all the ATMs in the world.

Vader would get no mercy from the hackers, so he showed his baby none.

He glanced in her direction and found Todd looking over her shoulder, though she was so engrossed she apparently didn't sense his presence.

Giving Brice a glance that appeared bland, but didn't feel that way to Brice, Todd went back to his own station where the guts of a computer were strewn across the table. Yet the area right in front of him was laid out like a surgeon's as he worked on a hard drive.

Strange dude, but if Jen thought so much of him, Todd must be brilliant, so he had to cut him some slack.

Yeah, and she has yet to think you're brilliant. Brice let out a bark of laughter, loud enough for both Todd and Jen to glance his way, making him chuckle more.

"Sorry, just had a thought that hit my funny bone."

Todd rolled his eyes and went back to work. Jen smiled and stretched.

"Got it. That one was tough, but Vader was able to keep up."

"Excellent. I can't wait to read the logs. This was an important attack." Brice had spent most of his military career controlling, learning about, and fighting the bad guys with a computer that barely kept up with the speed that everything changed. Few people realized just how much was run by computers and that global cyber terrorism was a major threat. Which was okay, because people like him did know. He and Jen worked to keep the bad guys at bay.

It was a good feeling to know he and Ms. Jennifer Malone were working together to help keep the world running a bit smoother, from ATMs that kept dispensing dollars to downloading a favorite book.

"Oh, no, what time is it?" Jen twisted around to look at her monitor's clock.

Brice glanced at his watch, a graduation gift from his dad. Very old school and he loved it. "Five forty-five."

"Crap, we're late. I'm always late," Jen wailed. "Can we shut down for now?"

"Sure."

"What are we late to?" Todd asked.

Brice looked around, and Todd was locking up his station as well.

"Annie is having Brice and me over for dinner," Jen clarified, apparently realizing Todd thought he too was invited.

That was the second time today she'd had to specifically exclude him from an invitation. What was Brice missing? Why would Todd think that?

Shrugging it off, Brice shut down his computer as did Jen.

Brice followed Todd out the lab's door and Jen set the code. On the ground floor they trooped to the parking lot, where a Porsche Cayenne SUV sat next to Jen's SUV. Brice's jaw hung open when Todd opened its doors. "Nice taste in cars."

For the first time Brice saw Todd actually smile. It was subtle, but his lips were definitely turned upwards. "My first goal was to own a Porsche, and with Colorado winters, this seemed the most logical."

"What's your second goal?"

"I don't have one yet. I'm pretty happy just the way things are."

Wouldn't that be a nice state of life to be in?

Brice was working toward that himself, and maybe was even close. Adding Jen to his circle might go a long way to making his life complete.

5
_____

JEN WAS A BIT ANXIOUS ABOUT ANNIE MEETING BRICE. OR maybe it was that Annie knew her so well that she'd see right through the already crumbling charade that Jen had been using to keep Brice at arm's length.

Indeed, she was impressed with Brice Young: he was smart, funny, damned good looking, more so now in street clothes, and with hair that was on the verge of being too long for her normal tastes. And the fact that he gave as good as he got almost made him perfect.

Except for the one flaw.

He was divorced.

Crazy, she knew, to let that bother her, especially in this day of easy no-fault divorces where the flimsiest excuse could be used to end a marriage. But Brice had left one marriage after a short stint, so why wouldn't he get out of another if it didn't quite meet his needs?

God, woman, you're not going to marry Brice. So lighten up.

Yeah, but then there were my so-called parents, and their

divorce, and don't forget Frederick and his charming slip of the tongue.

Remember, it's easier if you just stay away from all things related to the heart.

"Right."

"Excuse me?"

She looked at him, realizing she'd spoken out loud and hoped it had been only that word. "Right turn. Here." And hoped that covered her slip.

As she pulled into Annie's driveway, Brice let out a low whistle. "Boy, this Annie of yours knows how to celebrate the season."

"Pretty awesome isn't it? Annie's lights are a favorite in the city, and her lighting ceremony draws huge crowds that seem to grow each year."

"Ceremony? As in switching them on?"

"Exactly. Plus she gives out cider, and this year it snowed almost on cue."

They got out of the SUV, and Jen pointed to the lit stars in the tall Linden tree, looking as if they'd just fallen there. "Those are new this year."

"Pretty perfect for the lady that writes about stars and wishes coming true."

"I didn't tell you that."

"Nope, but if she's this special to you, I wanted to know a bit more about her, so looked her up."

Jen stopped dead in her tracks. Damn, if that wasn't one more tick in the plus column for the man. She quickly shook her head.

"What? I shouldn't have looked her up?"

The door opened. "Shouldn't have looked who up?" Annie said.

Jen rushed to give her a hug. "Merry Christmas, love."

The moment Annie's arms went around her, Jen felt like she'd come home. There was nothing like friends who were almost like sisters and had been close all their lives. "You. I was bragging on you, and Brice wanted to know what made you so special. Brice Young, Annabelle Hamilton."

"Annie, please. Nice to meet you."

Brice held out his hand, and Jen watched as Annie solemnly shook it, then before he could let go, pulled him into the house.

Jen let out her held breath. Brice passed the first Annie test.

He whistled again when he stepped past the foyer and spied her Christmas tree.

"I had the same first impression," a man's voice said from behind them.

"Cole Evans," he said. "And these are my boys, Peter and Josh."

The boys stepped forward and shook Brice's hand.

"Nice to meet you all. Thanks for including me in your dinner invitation, Annie."

"Annie makes the best mashed potatoes, and we're having some tonight because they're my favorite," Josh said.

Brice laughed and won another keen look from Annie. "I'm a potato man myself. Love 'em and can never seem to get enough."

"Wanna taste now?"

Brice nodded.

Josh was about to lead the way into the kitchen when he stopped and turned around. "Can we, Annie? Taste them?"

"Sure, you know where the spoon is. Be careful, the pan is hot," she directed the last bit toward Brice, who got the message.

"I like lots of butter on them..." Josh's voice trailed off.

Jen noticed that Cole and Peter followed them in. A moment later, she craned her neck to see Brice eating from the spoon Josh held to his mouth. It looked like they were having fun. Family fun. Something she'd never been interested in. At least not with a family of her own. She'd done just fine with Annie and Doc Hamilton, until Doc passed away several years ago.

"Ah-hem."

Jen pulled her gaze from the homey scene in the kitchen. "What?"

"Didn't you say once that you never wanted to see this man again?"

"Did I say that?"

Annie blinked twice, then crossed her arms and leaned against the door. "Yes."

"So what about you and Cole? I've been gone three days and it looks like things are very merry around you all."

"Don't change the subject—" Annie abruptly stopped talking, and Jen put on her best not-a-care-in-the-world face.

"Hold it. You've never done that before—well, not since college and Timmy Hart actually asked you to go away for the weekend, and you wouldn't tell me a thing until you got back."

"It was awful, too. What a puffer fish that boy was."

"So?"

"Later, okay?"

"How much later?" Annie asked in a whisper and glanced toward the kitchen. Cole was approaching with two glasses of wine.

"Tonight later," Jen whispered back and smiled radiantly at Cole, who was followed by Brice and his new-found friends, the boys.

"Did you know Brice was in the Air Force? And even knows how to fly a jet?" Peter said.

Brice laughed and Jen watched as even Annie melted at the deep, rich tone. "A plane with twin engines, but no jet."

"That's okay, you can fly!"

"We're going to look through my new telescope this evening. Want to come too?" Josh asked, giving Annie, then Jen his most winning smile.

Her heart melted just a tiny bit more. "You got a telescope for Christmas?"

"Yeah, because of Annie. I want to study stars."

Brice tilted his head and studied her best-est friend. Jen wondered what he was thinking, but sensed it was admiration. That was good because no matter how wonderful the man, if Annie and said man didn't approve of each other, said man was out of the picture.

"What if you all make tonight a guy night. I promise Jen and I will join you another night."

"Promise?" Josh looked first at Annie, then at her.

"You bet," she said, knowing this boy had a future as a first-class heart melter.

"Dinner's ready if you didn't eat all the potatoes," Annie said, earning a grin from Peter. "Take your seats and I'll serve."

"Need some help?" Brice asked.

"Nope, Peter beat you to it."

Peter? Jen was surprised, albeit pleasantly. Cole's older son had been very reluctant to embrace anything about Annie until she won a small victory against his defenses with her chocolate chip cookies. Granted the boy's uncle, Mitch, didn't help in any way. The poor man was still grieving for his sister, Cole's wife, gone for, what did Annie say? About two years now? But who wouldn't love Annie? And she seemed to have won a few more battles in the short number of days Jen had been gone. Maybe Annie'd wished on one of her stars.

And maybe Jen should do the same.

Wish for what? Brice? He had to reconstruct his life, not only as a single male, but to make the transition from ranking officer to civvie. For goodness sake, according to him, he lived in a barely habitable apartment. She didn't need to housetrain an adorable, big, gray-eyed puppy.

"Jen?"

She blinked at looked around the table. The boys were snickering and Cole's lips were upturned. Jen turned to

Brice to see him holding a huge casserole pan filled with bacon-and onion-stuffed meat rolls.

"Oh, yes, sorry. Sheesh, Annie, you actually made rouladen?" She served herself, and Brice put the heavy serving dish on a trivet in the center of the table.

"Yeah, she told us about it this morning, and we bugged her until she promised to make it tonight," Peter said.

"Guess what's for dessert?" Josh chimed in.

Jen poured some of the rouladen jus over her potatoes, but knew she'd better answer the boy before she dug into the feast. "Ice cream?"

"Yeah, with special chocolate sauce and nuts."

"Whipped cream?" Jen licked her lips.

"Sure, you have to have whipped cream," Cole said with a smile.

Jen grinned as Annie positively beamed. She couldn't wait to have a tête-à-tête with her buddy. What on earth had changed?

BRICE KEPT GLANCING AT JEN THROUGHOUT DINNER. SHE WAS charming, beautiful, and darn if he didn't want her. In the kitchen, chopping and cooking together. Working side by side in the business they both loved. In his bed, writhing beneath him, his lips trailing down that sleek body, his hand fisted in her hair.

Not again, old boy, not again. Rein it in. Feeling displaced and raging hormones do not mix well.

Still, the image of her in so many different facets of his life wouldn't disappear.

Jen laughed at something one of the boys said, and Brice wouldn't have thought she could be so at ease around them, but she was. She laughed with them, knew about their games, and if she didn't know something, wasn't afraid to ask. Only to have the two try and outdo each other with their answers to her.

She pushed back her hair and then twisted it up and stuck a chopstick through it that Annie had put by her plate. They must be best friends to have that type of intimate knowledge.

Brice watched as she sipped from her wine glass, the pull at his groin reminding him of the droplet of merlot clinging to her lip three nights ago in DC.

His move was completely out of character, yet it had been one of most intense experiences of his life. And seemed eons ago, not just days.

Jen met his eyes just as she put her glass on the table, and damned if the movies didn't have it right—the room narrowed to just the two of them. The shining curls of hair tucked up glinted from the modern crystal chandelier overhead. Tendrils escaped to curl around her face, and her whiskey-colored eyes gleamed with the shared memory.

Had they been alone, he would have pulled her onto his lap and started nibbling that delicate arch of neck above the white cowl-necked sweater. And if she didn't push him away, he might slide his hand beneath that fuzzy sweater—

"Nuts! I love peanuts. Do you want some too, Brice?" Peter asked.

He blinked and realized he'd pulled the same zone-out as Jen had a bit ago. "Yeah, I love all kinds of nuts. Including you two guys."

The boys' laughter filled the space that a millisecond ago had been almost an erotic dream. And at a dinner table with people he'd just met!

Quickly glancing at his hostess and her man, he saw the knowledge of what he'd been dreaming about reflected in Annie and Cole's eyes. He'd have to ask Jen just how long the two of them had been together.

Peter put a big bowl of vanilla ice cream in front of him. Hot fudge cascaded down the mound, topped with what looked like homemade whipped cream and chopped nuts. This was enough for the entire group.

He glanced around and each person had a bowl the same size, so this was his. He dipped a finger into the fluffy mound of white, brought it to his mouth, and almost drooled. It *was* home-whipped cream, with a hint of Madagascar vanilla just like his mom used.

Then Annie put down a platter of chocolate chip cookies.

"I'm gonna need a workout after this feast."

"I've got a home gym. Come over any time," Cole offered.

"Deal."

"Can we take a cookie with us for star watching?" Peter asked.

"I've got a bag ready for you," Annie said, as the boys

pushed back from the table, anxious to start their new adventure.

"Okay, I'm on dishes duty, who wants to help?" Brice said in his best military voice.

"We do, we do," the boys yelled in unison.

"No, you guys do your star gazing, and I'll do the dishes while Annie puts her feet up. After all, she has a dishwasher, and everything but the knives, pans and crystal can go in. Skedaddle." Jen shooed them out.

Brice stopped her as she headed into the kitchen. "I can help."

"I know, and you're good at it, but really, go be with the menfolk so Annie and I can catch up."

He held onto her arm a bit longer and leaned closer. "Are you going to gab about me?" he whispered, and fought the urge to nibble that curve of soft skin right under her ear.

"You bet, and stop that, you're tickling my ear."

"I know. I like it."

Jen pulled back a bit. "I don't."

"Liar."

"No I'm not."

"Yes, you are, I saw your eyes soften to near liquid."

"You're crazy, my eyes never do that."

"Yes, they do. And I'm betting they'll do it again."

Those same eyes widened with shock, and as he looked deeper he saw just a hint of anticipation.

"Spill it, we don't have to wait until the dishes are done. What's with Cole? It looks pretty cozy." Jen wasn't above badgering her best friend, and she wasn't kidding when she said this thing with Cole Evans looked much more permanent that it had before she'd left.

And that was what, only three days ago?

Haven't you completely changed your opinion of Brice in that short time span as well?

Annie put down the dish rag and whirled around. All of a sudden, Jen was pulled into a tight hug and swept around in a happy dance.

"You've moved beyond lust, I gather. Is it L.O.V.E?" Jen spelled out.

"Yep, and Cole loves me. Even the boys are coming around."

This time Jen twirled Annie twice in a tight circle, then hugged her close. "So I noticed. Have you set the date yet? A ring?"

Annie started laughing and soon tears were streaming down her cheeks. "Only you would ask, but no, and no. We are getting married, but when is the question. Brice looks pretty smitten with you. So..." Annie drew out the word. "We could have a double wedding."

Jen flicked her with the dish towel. "Remember that whole friends-with-benefits idea you came up with? That might be a thing I could manage with Brice, but no marriage."

"Wait, you never mix biz with pleasure."

"And I won't this time. General Cartwright wants the beta testing done by January first. So our partnership is short lived. By the way, how cool is this, the Air Force flew us out on one of their private jets."

"Very. And you're changing the subject. Anyway didn't you say Brice was military?"

"Not any longer."

"Since when?"

"I'm guessing within the last month. I'm not completely sure, but he did say his ex-wife won't be getting any of his retirement."

"Whoa, back up. He's divorced?"

"That's generally what 'ex' means," Jen said carefully, knowing Annie was going to grill her on this since Jen had been affected by it so early in her life.

But then so had Annie. *And she's not worried about getting married.*

Annie's mom, who'd left them when Annie was a young girl, was a divorcee when she'd married Adam Hamilton. Then when life got to be too much, too boring in Maine, she simply upped and left. Doc Hamilton's love and her daughter weren't enough to keep her.

And then there were Jen's parents, who fought all the time while married and after their divorce, Jen had been a pawn and often the bone they fought over for custody. Not because they wanted her, but because she was simply another irritant they could harass each other with.

Doc Hamilton had been Jen's real father and mentor, a kind and brilliant man who was never enamored of his status, only that he could help, heal, and offer an ear if nothing else was needed.

He was the one Jen thought of when Brice mentioned that General Cartwright was his mentor.

So she braced herself for her bestie's comments, wondering what her own reply would be. She was never anything but honest with Annie.

"You must have stronger feelings for Brice than anyone since...Frederick."

That's not what she expected. Leaning against the counter, kneading the dish towel between her fingers, Jen pursed her lips, then nodded. "You can't mention Frederick and Brice in the same sentence. Ugh. Brice is totally the opposite of what I thought he'd be like. He's funny, thoughtful, gives as good as he gets, and even sort of gets along with Todd."

"Whoa, now that is amazing," Annie said with a grin.

"Isn't it? I don't think Todd knows what to make of Brice yet. As you know, people tend to dismiss my number one assistant or talk down to him. Brice just went with the flow."

"You're stalling."

"Yeah, okay. He fell for this woman named Bethany, who apparently wanted a man in uniform. The breakup came, I think, when he told her he wasn't staying in any longer than his career retirement. He gave her the house, the car, but not his pension and no part of Vader. The house has a mortgage, the car is a couple of years old. And all he wants is the grand piano."

"He plays?"

"Apparently. I have yet to hear this for myself. I wonder where I could take him to play."

"Hello? The Boulderado's lobby. RJ's your buddy and would let him play."

Jen leaned over and hugged Annie. "Brilliant."

"Well, frankly I'm a bit worried about you. You're becoming twitter-pated and your brain's going to mush if you forgot RJ and the hours we've spent listening to him play."

Jen cuffed her on the shoulder as the image of leaning against the piano, wine glass in hand, listening to Brice play filled her mind. Pretty darn nice image too.

"You seem to know a lot about him so far."

"Not really, I don't know anything about his family, and he knows nothing about mine."

"Okay, since you say you're not mixing business with pleasure, tell me where the man is sleeping."

Jen grinned. "The lab at the house."

Annie's jaw dropped. "He's staying with you?"

"Yep, not really my choice, but then I didn't argue too strenuously against it. I haven't told him about the guest suite."

"Oh, you're bad."

"I know, but at the time, my hands were tied, so telling him the lab was the only place to sleep happened to be the one way I felt I had control. Enough of me—what about Cole."

Annie blushed. "Well, obviously we love each other, and the boys were easy to fall for. Josh, immediately. Peter took a bit more time."

"What about Mitch?"

"I think Lauren's brother realizes that Cole is moving

forward, and that it's healthier for the boys if their uncle doesn't keep resurrecting the pain of everyone's lost love. Nobody wants to let Lauren's memory die," Annie said with a beseeching look.

Jen gathered her into another hug. "Of course not. You're not taking Lauren's place."

"No, I'm not. Honestly, all this is so new to us, we're just taking it step by step."

"I'm right there with you, sister, swimming in my own uncharted waters."

Annie laughed. "I think you mixed your metaphors. Will you be my Maid of Honor?"

"Do you even have to ask? Just don't make it a horrible bridesmaid's dress, promise?" Jen said hugging Annie.

6

"WHOA, THAT IS WAY COOL, DAD," JOSH SAID. "YOU CAN even see the lines on the planet's surface."

"My turn," Peter said, stomping his feet with what Brice guessed was both impatience and cold.

They'd set up the telescope in an open space in the middle of Chautauqua Park above Cole's house. It surprised Brice that Cole lived next door to Annie, and he wondered how long they'd been together as it was obvious from the looks and soft touches throughout dinner that they were deeply in love.

It had been a quick half-block walk up from Cole's house to the park, and there was enough open sky to get a great view.

If Brice had still had on his loafers, he'd have frostbite by now, but luckily he fit more or less into an extra pair of Cole's boots.

Finally Josh moved aside so his brother could have his turn.

"Wicked," Peter said, glued to the eyepiece of the scope.

"Jupiter is my favorite planet," Josh said fervently.

What a cute kid. Brice hadn't thought much about wanting or not wanting kids, but when Bethany got pregnant, the decision was made. He was going to be a dad.

Then he wasn't. It was the beginning of the end, had he known it.

He wondered what Jen thought about kids. Then he shook his head, pushing away the quick thought. That was way too personal a question to ask this soon.

He focused back on the kids with him right now. "Wait until you see Saturn, Josh. That's my favorite," he said.

"When does it come up so can we see it?" Peter turned to his father.

"I'm not sure, but we can get some star apps and find out," Cole said.

Brice noticed that Josh was trying to hide his shivering —the major drawback with stargazing in winter. "Hey, I know it's your first time using your new telescope, but I think I'm going to have call it a night." He pretended to shiver violently. "Next time I'll come more prepared, that is, if you'll invite me again."

"You bet you can come, right, Dad?" Josh asked.

"Any time," Cole agreed. "Let's all pack it in, and we'll do it again tomorrow night if it works. Meanwhile, we'll get some star charts."

"I bet Annie has some."

"Good thinking, we'll ask her, and meanwhile your brother can do a search for some apps. Okay Pete?"

"Sure."

Cole grabbed the scope and Brice grabbed the chairs. "We have to let the scope warm up and make sure it's dry before we put it away," he told his sons.

Trooping down the block and into the house, Brice followed the boys as they ran into the living room. In less than a minute the boys were sitting next to each other, heads touching, as Pete worked his iPad to look for apps. "Hey, Dad, there's a bunch of cool ones—look."

Cole and Brice stood behind the couch, looking at the screen. Brice leaned over and pointed to one. "I use this one to find the planet and stars location. When I was your age, I used a cardboard chart that you dialed around to find what was showing, and approximately when. Now it's all real-time coordinates."

"Cool. You still stargaze?" Peter asked him.

"Sure, I love finding the stars and planets or watching meteor showers," he said, and meant it. Kansas, with its lack of light pollution, was perfect for spending hours with an eye glued to the scope.

"I'm going to head back to Annie's and grab Jen. Thanks for letting me be part of your first stargazing party." Brice held his hand out to Cole. "Thanks for the boots. I gotta get some tomorrow."

Cole walked him to the door, and Brice looked back to make sure they were out of earshot of the boys. "You've got great kids. And Annie? Wow!"

"Don't I know. Lauren died a little over two years ago,

and I never thought I'd fall in love again. And as for Jen, you'd have your hands full, but what a kick it could be."

"Think I'm aiming to find out." Brice left the warmth of Cole's house and boots, and immediately felt the cold. Nevertheless, he stood on the sidewalk for a few moments, looking at Annie's display of lights and thinking about Jen.

Life would never be dull around Jennifer Malone.

7

JEN GROPED HER WAY INTO THE DARK KITCHEN, NOT believing she was up at four-thirty in the morning. She definitely didn't want to turn on the lights and blind her already tired eyes, but she needed coffee badly and told herself for the millionth time that she was becoming an addict and should, at the very least, cut back if not cut the caffeine out altogether.

But not now, not with the crucial beta testing going on and Brice around her all the time, making her feel like she needed to be on her toes.

She turned on the machine, thankful she'd filled it with beans and water last night. And within minutes, took her first sip, blessing the brew.

Staring across the dark yard to her lab, she wondered if Brice slept any better than she did.

Of course he did, you ninny. He'd not angsting over anything. He may have an itch he needs to scratch, but questioning himself about it? No. He probably slept like the proverbial rock.

And what did he sleep in? Boxers, sweats, jammies... nothing? That last image nearly caused her to spit out her coffee. Long legs, strong chest, slim hips. Not an ounce of fat on him from what she could see. And she sure wanted to see the rest.

Then, in a purely feminine way, she wondered what Brice thought of her figure? She patted her own flat tummy, remembering the enormous bowl of ice cream she'd had last night. With extra whipped cream no less. Maybe she should work out with Brice at Cole's home gym.

Oh my God. Exercise? *You don't even know what the term means.*

True, but she could learn, right? And she was sure Brice would help her just as she'd help him learn to use a knife. Body next to body, straining with the weights. Hand on top of hand, slicing through the firm skin of a tomato...

STOP!

Deliberately making herself turn away from the view of her lab and the hot, sensuous images of who was sleeping in it, she made another cup of coffee and took it back to her bedroom.

The caffeine was kicking in, so another couple of hours of sleep was out of the question. She'd shower, dress and recall Vader's data and make notes on what the beast could do. That was the solution to waiting until Brice woke up.

Forty-five minutes later, dressed in jeans, her most favorite boots, mid calf, brown leather with fleece, and a white silk shirt topped by a red wool vest, she was sitting at her kitchen counter, this time with the lights on.

Cradling her third cup as she jotted observations about Vader, she saw a beam of light heading her way. Brice was up before the sun as well.

Good, they'd grab bagel sandwiches from Moes and get to the office early.

She started a cup for him as he entered the back door, using the key she gave him last night.

Jen had fought herself over the question of giving him a key, then just what to say so it didn't seem like an invitation into her bed. Which it wasn't.

Really, it wasn't.

She'd decided it was best to simply tell him to use it in case she was unavailable to let him in. Simple, clean and factual. Jen kept her face straight and even tried to put a bit of iciness into her voice. That part had failed spectacularly, and Brice had noticed. The smile wasn't on his lips, but it lit up his eyes.

Another reason she didn't sleep well last night.

Two more steps and he took the cup from her hand and smiled his thanks. As he drank, she took in his bleary eyes. "Didn't sleep well last night?"

Despite the obvious bags under his eyes, his grin was brilliant, megawatts strong. "Had a lot on my mind."

As did I.

His grin widened as if he'd read her mind.

"You know, Vader and all that," he said.

She caught herself just as her jaw began to drop. "Yep,

me too, thinking about work," she patted the pad where she jotted notes.

Brice glanced at the notes, then picked up the pad and concentrated on them. "Yeah, you got it. We can't hack back the hackers, but thankfully we can trace them. Though most know how to bury their trail, as we discovered yesterday. We're looking for bigger fish than the 'Script Kiddies.'"

Jen laughed. "I haven't heard that term in a while."

He smiled. "Were you a Script Bunny in school?"

"I beg your pardon? That's sexist, and an insult." Jen rested her hands on hips and cocked a hip. But ruined the effect with the chuckle she couldn't suppress. "But seriously, I never wanted to be a Script Kiddie or Bunny and use someone else's malicious software to attack computer networks. Showing off that way was something I'd never do. Anyway, I'd design my own program if I wanted to be a hacker.

"Still, I don't think you should dismiss the "skiddies" of either sex. After all, they created the huge denial of service that shut down those online retailers and cost them millions."

"I'm not dismissing them. That would be foolish. But frankly Vader is going to be way too expensive for mom and pop operations, and there are plenty of other defense systems to handle the skiddies or the hacktivists. As long as there are computers—"

"There will be someone wanting in," she finished for him. "Let's go to work."

"I'LL BET YOU A BEVERAGE OF YOUR CHOICE AT THE Boulderado that Todd will be at work before we are," Brice said. "And since I'm going to win, I'm ordering another bagel for him."

Jen leaned against the counter at Moe's as they waited for their bagel sandwiches. "You're on. Neither Susan or Todd are early risers and since they work pretty much on their own schedule unless we have a team project, who in their right mind would come in early on a day like today?"

She pointed out the window. The white stuff was falling again.

"There's nothing I like more than to sleep in on a gray snowy day. Or read the paper in bed with a cup of coffee." As if punctuating her words, she stretched, letting loose a big yawn.

Brice barely bit down his sigh. Why did she have to mention that? He really did need to rein in his all-too-vivid imagination.

Their order was ready. He grabbed the bags and led the way out the door. Anything to take his mind off images of Jen, tousled and warm in a cozy bed with cold snow falling outside.

JEN PARKED IN HER DESIGNATED SPOT, AND THIS EARLY, HERS was practically the only car in the garage.

Except for a Porsche Cayenne.

Brice really hadn't wanted to win their bet, not that he disliked the guy. It was that he really wanted to work alone with Jen. But something about Todd told him he'd be at the office waiting for them.

Brice exchanged a glance with Jen.

"Okay, okay, you win."

"After we eat these," he held up the Moe's bags, "and run the next test, I need to get boots," Brice said, as they walked out of the parking garage.

"There's a great store just down the block. It'll have what you need."

Jen swiped her card, and they entered the lab of ForceOne.

Todd was already at his station, his evidence locker open and work spread across his desk.

He turned. "Moes?" he said hopefully, looking at Brice holding the bag.

"Yeah, and Brice actually had the thought about getting you one. I didn't think you'd be here this early, but he did."

"Thanks, Major...err, Brice."

"You're welcome."

"I'm just finishing up the last of the case work, checking my notes and the data," he said to Jen.

"Good. We'll go over it after I've completed Vader's vetting," Jen said, punctuating her words with a warm smile.

Todd beamed at both of them and returned to his workstation, bagel in hand.

Brice caught Jen's attention and mimicked holding up a

beer glass to his lips, then got his own warm—no, make that hot—smile in return.

Jen didn't have any idea how incredibly sexy she could be without trying. Because he didn't really think she was trying to be sexy in her own office, in front of her employee.

He sat at the conference table with her, and even after that gargantuan meal last night, he wolfed several bites of his bagel with bacon and Swiss. Then needed coffee to wash it down.

Just as he pushed back his chair to make a couple of cups of the brew, a steaming cup was placed in front of Jen, perpendicular to her right hand. Then one for him, again precisely placed.

"Thanks, Todd." Jen sipped hers.

"I second that," Brice said, completely surprised. Maybe Todd just needed to feel like Brice hadn't been taking over his spot on the team. Whatever it was, the atmosphere in the lab felt less hostile. In fact, he'd call it down right comfortable. A camaraderie that happened rarely with a group of experts. His usual experience was the opposite, where one-upmanship reigned.

"By the way, Annie texted me this morning," Jen said, interrupting his thoughts. "And you're a hit with the boys. They can't wait to go stargazing again. Cole was singing your praises as well."

Just then the lab's door opened, and a tall, lean redhead walked in. Short, sleek hair—one side cut shorter than the other—cupped her face. This vision wore a long black coat that swept the ground as she walked and had a dusting of snow about three inches deep around the hem.

"Hey, everybody, how was Christmas? And who are you?" she asked as she approached the coffee station.

Her voice was husky and way too sensual for an office setting.

Brice stood and held out his hand. "Brice Young, working with Jen on a beta test. I'm guessing you're the third member of the ForceOne troika?"

Susan glanced Jen's way with a raised brow. "As in Major Brice Young?"

"Retired," Brice said.

The vision laughed, low and throaty. "Too funny, Jen. We have a sergeant as in Todd Sargent and a major—albeit retired in our office."

Brice groaned, but couldn't keep smile off his lips.

She slipped off her coat to reveal a very snug black sweater over skin-tight black pants and tall black boots. "Susan Hancock. Nice to meet you."

Susan held out her hand, and he noticed a tattoo encircling her wrist. Grasping her long white fingers, he turned her wrist and noticed the tat was an intertwined design of zeroes and ones. The basis of computing. "Very devoted to your job?"

"I've always had a love affair with computers. I wrote code when I was a kid, and believe it or not, I tried hacking into the social security administration," Susan said. "Didn't get far and figured I'd better turn to the other side."

"Never. I'll never turn to the Dark Side," Brice quoted

"God, really? A Sweek?"

"A what?"

"Star Wars Geek."

"Then that I am."

He looked around to realize Jen and Todd both stared at him. Disbelief was the predominate emotion he read in each stare. Palms up, he shrugged. "I yam what I yam."

Groans came from all three.

"I can do more."

"Please don't," was the chorus.

Brice put on a very dejected face, following it with a grin. "Nice to meet you, Susan."

"Mutual I'm sure." Susan said with a nasal twang

"White Christmas? Barrie Chase playing Doris Lenz?" Brice couldn't hold back his laugh.

"Bingo. You're good." Susan said.

"Can we get back to work?" Jen asked, laughter erasing the substance of her request.

"Of course." Brice pulled his laptop from its case and started keying in passwords. Computer ready to go, he glanced up, and saw the smile still tugging at Jen's lips.

"Always been a movie nut," he said.

"I used to love movies, just ran out of time."

The yearning in her voice nearly had him shutting off the computer, grabbing her hand and heading to the nearest theater. "I make the time."

Her casual shrug belied the longing written on her face. Didn't Jen ever just play? Slip away from the job once in a while to recharge her batteries?

Brice couldn't ask her, not here at work. And since Susan and Todd were now at their stations working, and

Jen's fingers were poised over her keyboard, waiting for him, it was time to get to work.

He keyed a few commands into the computer. "Okay, you're on, I've just started the attack."

The only noise in the office was the clicking of keys, the whir of the coffee machine and an occasional, "nailed you again, you bastard" from Susan.

Brice checked the time, worried that so much time had passed with Jen not saying a word. Was Vader working? This was a tough attack and he thought he'd fixed the issues that had caused his system to fail this test the first time through.

"Okay, it got it. That one was rough, I thought Vader hung up for a moment, out of RAM or something, but he was just thinking," Jen said, then chuckled. "God, aren't we sad, talking about machines as if they have a gender and are alive."

"I was getting worried there. It's been four hours—"

"I count my time by coffee and I know I had four cups. Thanks for that."

"Wasn't me. Todd beat me each time. Don't know how he does that."

Todd swiveled his chair around from his station. "It's just a matter of counting how many times you pick up the cup. Jen drinks faster than you. Yours got cold. I tossed out the old and refreshed the cup."

Brice blinked. "How do you do that with your back turned?"

Lifting a shoulder, Todd swiveled back to his work, as if embarrassed by the attention.

"However you do it, thanks. And since we're done, and before I check the logs to see what Vader was doing when it was thinking, how about lunch and boots."

"You're on. Anybody want anything?" Jen asked Todd and Susan.

Susan just waved her hand, not looking up from her work, while Todd deliberated, then shook his head no. Brice shouldered his computer case and Jen locked up hers.

Lunch was a bowl of soup and a sandwich at the West End Tavern, then on to boot shopping.

THE PEDESTRIAN SHOP WAS FILLED WITH ALL MANNER OF footwear, almost too much for Brice to take in as he stood in the middle of the store, turning in a circle. "Take pity on me. Point to something."

"Snow boots, right?"

"Yep, and they have to be warm if I'm going to do any more night astronomy."

Jen pointed to a wall of Columbia boots. "You really enjoyed that, didn't you?"

"Yeah, I did. I didn't have that kind of scope as a kid, but Dad took me out, and then my sister got interested, so Mom, being the good sport as she is, got interested too. It became a family affair."

"Did you want to be an astronaut?"

The saleswoman brought out the boots. Brice tried

them on and instantly his feet felt warm. "Sold, I'm going to wear them."

The clerk put his loafers in the box and led them to the cashier's desk.

Brice handed over his credit card and, while waiting for the transaction to go through, answered Jen.

"Yes and no. Basically I decided I liked computer work better, and although the science was interesting, I realized I really wasn't cut out to do that."

"Why?"

"Don't tell anyone, promise?"

"Sure, I think."

Brice gave her a stern look.

She crossed her heart.

"I get G-force sick. Can't even fly in a fighter jet, let alone handle what a rocket would do to me."

Jen laughed so loud the other patrons in the store glanced their way. "Your secret is safe with me. No one would believe me if I told them the uber cool Major Young gets air sick."

"Excuse me, it's G-force sick."

"Right."

As Brice held open the door to the store for Jen to exit, Dom Pauly entered. Jen's heart sank. She'd helped Dom as a favor to a man she'd dated, and now Dom turned to her if he couldn't get immediate action on any small computer issue. Thankfully she was usually out of town when he called. Hopefully he'd just say hi and move on.

"Hey, perfect timing. Did you get my call?"

"Hi, Dom. No, sorry. I'm in the middle of a project, so I'm not taking phone calls." She hoped the man would get the drift.

"Oh. Well, I really need your help, so it's a good thing I ran into you."

"Let's move out of the doorway," Brice said smoothly, but Jen heard the exasperation in his voice. He understood immediately.

"Brice Young, Dom Pauly. He owns the jewelry store down the block," Jen introduced.

"Nice to meet you," Dom said. "Jen, the computer's down, it's our biggest sale of the year and my computer doc can't come out for a couple of days. I really need you."

"What's it doing?" Brice asked.

"Nothing," Dom's voice rose. "It's so slow. It's taking forever to process a sale. I'm losing customers."

Jen sighed inwardly. "Of course I'll help—"

"We'll help," Brice said.

Dom practically ran them to his store. It was packed and it was easy to see the frustration on his customer's unsmiling faces. In fact some people were walking out, head shaking.

"Hey, Dom, what gives?" one man yelled from across the store.

Dom pasted on a smile, and Jen felt his hand on her back, pushing her forward faster.

Once in his office, Jen took off her coat and opened the

closet that held the server. She looked at the logs and realized Dom hadn't followed her instructions from last time she'd helped.

"You didn't get the bigger hard drives?"

"No, I thought I could get through the season."

Jen pushed aside a tangle of wires. "Who's been working on this?"

"That computer doc I mentioned and my son, of course."

She'd heard Dom speak of his son and he was an expert in *everything*. Jen had no idea who the computer doc was that Dom spoke of as Boulder had a plethora of them.

"Hmm, I'm not going to touch the server. So let me study the logs for a minute and see if I can find a way to get you some speed."

"Thanks, Jen. I knew I could trust you to help. By the way, old Miss Hodges, Annie's neighbor? She's gonna take your next computer class. She came in to buy some earrings for her great granddaughter and told me. She was so proud of the fact. You do a good thing."

"Jen teaches classes?" Brice shifted so he could rest his hip on the desk.

She heard the surprise in Brice's voice and quickly looked down at the logs in her hands, too embarrassed to check out his expression. "I teach four times a year, the basics of windows, launching programs, what to do if you can't close a program. Basic stuff. It's nothing."

"Heck, Jen is being too modest," Dom said, poking Brice in the ribs. "A cum laude teaching the basics? And for free? That is something. In fact Jen scares me with her mind. I'll tell you a secret. I wanted to date her, but realized that would be a mistake. Too damn smart for me. We wouldn't have lasted a month, let alone a year or a lifetime."

Jen jerked up her head and met Brice's wide-eyed gaze with one of her own.

"Okay, this might work," she said, rushed, wanting nothing more than to escape. Dom's words were almost a copy of Frederick's breakup speech to her. *This relationship is a mistake. I'm getting out. I need to feel like I'm equal with you, and that's not happening. So better now than a divorce in a year."*

"I can't replace the hard drives or upgrade." Jen fought to keep her voice level, and not to choke on the tightness Dom's words caused. She was long over Frederick, realizing she was best out of that relationship. But just the concept that divorce was an easy way to erase a mistake echoed what Brice had said about his marriage.

"The only thing I can suggest is to shut down your desk-top computer in here," she said. "Keep only one register open to reduce the load on the hard drives and offer everyone a bigger discount today to keep them happy."

Dom didn't look excited at her discount idea.

"Good idea, Jen. I know my sister would be thrilled if that deal were offered by her favorite jewelry store," Brice said.

Those words brightened Dom's face. Jen put on her coat as the man shut down his computer. They followed him out to the store's sales floor and heard a bit of his announcement to his customers.

They got out, but not before they heard a cheer.

JEN SAT AT HER WORKSTATION, YET HER FINGERS REMAINED idle on the keyboard.

Shopping for Brice's boots, with the store still decorated with the lights and trees of the season made that small bit of shopping feel like Christmas. Jen instantly tried to picture Brice dealing with the crowds while doing his own holiday buying. She wondered if he was a cranky last-minute shopper or one who embraced the season and dealt easily with the chaos as part of the whole package.

She was an embracer. While she might not decorate much, it was her schedule that dictated that decision, not her heart. She loved the peace and hope that Christmas brought to the world.

A pang of longing twinged her soul. Christmas and New Year's were two holidays that needed to be shared with someone you loved. To wake up with the anticipation of Christmas morning in the arms of your lover. To ring in the New Year with a kiss at midnight that promised being together in the coming year as surely as the ring on one's finger.

Brice could be all those things. She felt it in her bones, in her heart. It was her head that made the arguments at warp speed.

He'd failed at marriage once.

Why assume he'd do it again? It sounded like it wasn't his fault.

Maybe. It's a risk I don't want to take. I couldn't bear to lose someone I loved because they wanted out.

That can happen with any marriage, not just because Brice is divorced.

True, but it was easy to get out once, why not again? That old adage has truth to it, you know. What if he just isn't willing to work on the problems if they come? Frederick wasn't.

And what if Brice is?

Jen let loose a sigh.

"That was a big one, boss," Susan said, two stations away.

Jen focused and glanced quickly at her employee in time to see the twinkle in her eyes, just before she turned back to her work.

"Only four days left in the year, and I gotta get this project done," Susan said to the room. "I've got big plans for New Year's."

"Do you have plans for New Year's," Brice whispered into Jen's ear.

She jumped, then turned her head toward his voice. Her mouth was way too close to Brice's. Pulling up her willpower, she scooted her chair back enough so the temptation to capture his lips in a soul-searing kiss was removed. "It depends on how much more Vader work we have to accomplish. What's yours?"

"This year, if it wasn't for Vader, I'd have been in Pasadena at the Rose Parade."

She stared at him. Luckily her jaw *didn't* drop this time. "What? Are you kidding?"

"No, baby sis has her first float in the parade this year—"

"Oh, cute, what float is she riding on?"

Brice let out the most delicious laugh yet, rumbling from his chest, exploding in a deep baritone. "I'm not going to tell her you said that," he finally got out between chuckles.

Jen was baffled by his attitude. "Why? It's a big honor to ride on a Rose Parade float."

"Because she builds the suckers. For the last five years she's engineered and built floats for Macy's and a couple of other parades, as well designed river barges for the San Antonio River Walk. This year is her first Rose Parade entry."

God, would the man ever stop surprising her? Her jaw had hung down more in the past four days than in the entire past year. Make that two years.

"Well, if we get done here in time, you can catch a jet and be there."

"You know, I think I'll stay in Boulder for New Year's."

He'd lowered his voice and whispered the simple phrase. Yet each word sounded deliciously sexy and filled with promise. She wanted to keep her distance, wanted to not be attracted to him.

Instead, heat crept up Jen's back, circled her tummy, then flooded her face. And damn if he didn't grin, knowing exactly what was happening to her.

"So what are you doing for the big night?" His gaze glinted with wicked mischief.

It was time for her to get even. "Usually I take a long, soaking bath with a bottle of champagne in an ice cooler next to the tub. The room lit by candle light and a bit of music on. It's my favorite way to spend New Year's."

It was all a lie, but the way Brice's Adam's apple bobbed, none of it mattered except retaliation for her own arousal. It was sweet to see him at a loss for words, more than a bit disconcerted, and even in a bit of pain if that bulge in his pants was any indication.

Jen looked over at Susan to see, although hunched over her desk, her shoulders shook with laughter. Jen was grateful she didn't have to meet her gaze.

And thankfully, super observant Todd had left for lunch.

8

Brice's gaze followed hers downward to the apex of his jeans, and while he wasn't at all keen that she noticed his obvious turn on, it served her right. Especially when the tip of her tongue poked through her lips as if she wanted to lick them.

Lick her lips, he told his unruly libido. Calm down.

"You really are a wicked woman," he whispered, then moved back to the conference table and managed to sit down.

Just then his cell phone rang. He checked caller ID and took the call. "Caro, how goes it?"

"Great, fantastic, I wish you could be here to see this. Any chance of finishing early and being here?"

"Okay, what's wrong, kiddo?"

The few moments of dead air told him she was grasping for the right words. Caroline was such an upbeat, energetic woman, he couldn't imagine what was going on. "Caro, is it Mom, Dad?"

"God, no—sorry, I didn't mean to scare you. I'm just overwhelmed and needed to hear your voice."

That wasn't normal. His sister was rarely overwhelmed with any task. "I'm all yours. Hey, did you get the waterfall to work without splashing the riders?"

"Yes, we built up the faux rocks, and covered them with moss so they don't splash back as much. It's a fun float, with all the jungle animals and birds. One rider is going to handle a boa."

He heard the shiver in her voice. "Are you walking the route with the float?"

"You bet. I want to see the crowd's reactions and see how the float moves."

"As if you didn't figure all that out already, I bet you have computer models with stress loads for sway and bounce."

She laughed and he felt better.

"Yeah, all of that, but still—"

"Honey, I know it's your biggie, and I know you're more than up to the challenge. You're going to have so many orders you'll get to pick and choose."

Caro laughed again and his lips curved in response.

"Okay, you've fixed me. Love you, big bro."

More dead air. She was done.

He disconnected.

A pang of something akin to homesickness flooded Brice. So many times his commitment to the military had to come first. Sure, he was usually able to schedule leave for important events, but the job came first. And now it was going to be like that again.

Not if you have the right people in your company.

He'd thought about that aspect day and night since he'd decided to leave the service and create Vader and start a business. He knew several fellow officers and non-coms he wanted and had already approached. Some of his chosen were available within weeks and others he'd have to wait on. But with Vader's price tag of three-quarters to a cool million including support, he needed the best.

Jen was the best, but he was pretty sure she wasn't going to abandon ForceOne.

Maybe Boulder was the city in which to headquarter his business. It had the technology base, the geeks to support it, and the lifestyle here was next to none. The mountains, skiing, hiking, camping. Close enough to a big international airport for worldwide tech support travel and enough surrounding communities for a range of housing options.

And then there was Jen.

Whoa, pull up the reins, big boy. You're not moving to a city because of a woman. Period.

His gaze was drawn to the woman in question. Her hair, tucked behind her ears, gave him a full view of her profile.

Classic.

Strong enough jaw, but not stubborn, though he knew she could dig in her heels with the best of them. A nose that was straight, and thankfully not perky. He couldn't see her eyes but didn't need to; those whiskey brown eyes were etched in his memory.

Jennifer Malone was a classy lady, from the top of her shining blonde head to the tips of her brown boots.

And he itched to make her more than a beta tester for him.

Slow down. Didn't you learn your lesson with Bethany?

He shivered, couldn't help it. Caroline had named his marriage "The Bethany Incident," spoofing the movie *The Ox-Bow Incident.*

His parents had refrained from making any comments. After all, he was a grown man and should have known better.

This summer his mom had been in DC for a few days of visiting and museum touring, and a dinner at General Mitchell's house. After she returned to Brice's tiny apartment, she'd confided to him that she wasn't the only one happy he was rid of Bethany. Mom had said in her mild way—with a hint of steel underlying each word—that he needed to find a smart woman he could keep up with.

A smart woman. Someone that would keep growing and moving side by side with him.

Bethany hadn't been that woman. Mom had met her only once, at the wedding, and had been sweet and welcoming. Bethany had been all gushy over her, but apparently his Kansas mom saw right through her from the start.

Jen, however, was a woman who he knew instinctively would be the type of person his family would approve of and bond with. They'd love her.

But he was putting everything on overdrive again.

Damn, he didn't even know if she already had a boyfriend. She hadn't mentioned one, although that meant nothing, Jen wasn't one to confide in a stranger, and he'd bet Annie was really her only confidant.

"Okay, done. I've got notes for you, but mostly they are simple little tweaks. Vader did what he was supposed to do," Jen said.

Brice blinked twice to pull himself into the present. "Great. I was worried after it took so long. Tomorrow, I'm going to run a 'low and slow' attack we don't have to monitor closely. Instead of twiddling our thumbs waiting for the beast to see if I, hacker extraordinaire, can beat it, I thought we'd go into the mountains and snowshoe. Have you ever been to Bear Lake in Rocky Mountain National Park?"

BRICE WANTED TO SNOWSHOE? JEN HADN'T DONE THAT IN what, ten plus years?

Living in Maine, she and Annie, along with Doc, would often snowshoe in the woods behind their house. They'd return to Annie and Doc's home, a steaming mug of apple cider waiting, followed by dinner sitting on the floor in front of their huge stone fireplace. It was homey, wonderful and loving.

"Of course I know Bear Lake. Do you know how to snowshoe?"

"It's been awhile," Brice admitted. "But Cole had

mentioned the boys and their recent outing, and it sounded fun."

"I don't have any equipment."

"Can't we rent it?" Brice said.

"Sure, but I think Annie has some. I'll call her."

"Okay either way. It sounds like a great way to blow out the cobwebs from being indoors. And since we're done for today earlier than I thought, let's start winding down with a drink."

Could Jen have asked for a better scenario? Someone must be looking out for her. "How about the Boulderado?"

"The Catacombs still there?"

"Gone. It's now License One, and yes, the hotel is still around.

"License One sounds a bit fancier than the old Catacombs. I fondly remember my time at the bar in the basement, and of course the Walrus."

"You weren't old enough to drink the hard stuff when you were at the Academy."

"Beer. Like I said, when we came up for football games, we didn't wander off campus much, except to the bars."

Jen shook her head. "Come on, we'll walk to the Boulderado, it's only a few blocks, and you have boots now." Jen turned to Susan. "You're not pulling an all nighter, are you?"

"Maybe, but Todd promised to help after he gets back from lunch, so hopefully not. Just as long as it's done by New Year's. This Campbell case is a doozy."

Jen nodded. "That will be an interesting trial if it gets that far. Bye."

It wasn't yet five, but Jen used the "it's five-o'clock somewhere" rationale and was pretty sure her buddy RJ would be at what he called "his office" at the Boulderado.

She'd had a couple of memorable first dates at the iconic hotel. Its Victorian decor, the stained glass atrium over the mezzanine that looked down into the lobby, and first class everything made it a romantic spot for a drink or dinner. She'd even had holiday tea in the mezzanine with Annie a few times.

Sadly, her second and rare third dates always petered out after the rush of initial attraction, and not even the Boulderado could make them better.

Not so with Brice. She'd spent four days around him, and he was still surprising her. It was fun keeping up with him.

They made the quick trek up the Pearl Street Mall, over to Thirteenth and a few blocks up to Spruce.

Luck was with her. RJ was sitting at the piano playing a few riffs, warming up.

Brice went to the Corner Bar in the lobby while Jennifer headed in the direction of the piano.

"RJ."

"Miss Jennifer," he returned in their usual greeting. "Anything you want me to play tonight?"

"I have a favor to ask. Do you think you could let my friend play for a few minutes?"

"He any good?"

"I'd like to find out."

"Well then, send him on over."

"Here he comes. Thanks, RJ," she said softly, watching Brice approach. Long legs ate the distance with a few strides. He held a tall glass of beer for himself and glass of white wine for her.

"Brice, meet RJ, a friend since I discovered the Boulderado."

He handed her the wine and stuck out his hand. "Nice piano you have here."

RJ got up, making a sweeping gesture toward the piano bench. "Give 'em a try," he said, and moved aside.

Jen caught the gleam in Brice's gray eyes. "I'm pretty rusty."

But he practically thrust his beer glass at Jen and sat. Wiping his hands on his pants, he ran a few scales, not missing a key.

"Nice," she said with a wink.

"Funny. Got that habit from Mom, town's piano teacher. Scales, more scales, minor, thirds, backwards. Had to do them constantly."

RJ was nodding with a smile. Jen thought this boded well for Brice's ability.

Then the man started tickling the keys in earnest, and Jen's eyes widened, and damn if her jaw didn't drop again. Brice was playing *Rhapsody in Blue* by Gershwin, one of her all-time favorite pieces from the 1920s.

"Got your answer, Miss Jennifer?" RJ whispered.

"Unbelievable."

A crowd was drawn to the music and Brice played on. It didn't matter that there wasn't the orchestral accompaniment, his fingers were nimble, and he understood the magic of the music.

If Jen ever allowed herself to fall in love, Brice would be at the top of the list. She could listen to him play every night before falling into bed with him and having those same magical fingers work their enchantment on her body.

Heat flowed from the tips of her toes, through all her vital parts, and she was sure steam seeped from her ears.

All in full view of everyone crowding around the piano.

Too soon he finished the piece, his fingers still, but they continued to rest on the keyboard.

She tried to avoid his gaze, a useless attempt, as his own zeroed in on her. Amidst the clapping, the people receded, then swirled around them in a haze as if the hotel's lobby held only the two of them.

JENNIFER MALONE NEVER LOOKED MORE ENTICING AS THEIR gazes met over the piano.

Brice was high from playing. It hadn't mattered that there were other people in the lobby, he played just for her. And now he wanted to sweep her up, carry her to a room upstairs and make long, slow love to her. To play his fingers over her body, learning each spot that made her whimper or cry out. To have her squirm beneath his touch.

He saw the same need in her eyes. But hidden deep in the whiskey depths was a bit of reserve he didn't understand. Something was holding her back. Someone or maybe several life lessons had been harsh to Jen. Brice wanted, no, needed to erase those memories and replace them with better ones.

And then what? Happily ever after?

Why not? He'd seen marriages that worked and wanted one of his own. His folks were still in love after forty plus years of the wedded state. General Mitchell and his wife still had the magic—it was in every touch they shared, whether on purpose or by accident.

Many of his buddies were happily married, a few not. But he didn't think any of them had been as stupid as he had with Bethany.

He didn't want to be stupid with Jen.

There was an undeniable chemistry between them. Even if she wanted to pretend otherwise, her body and her eyes said differently.

"Man, you can come and play any night," RJ said.

And the world intruded. "Thanks for letting me use your piano, it's a beaut."

"You got one somewhere?"

"Yeah, back in DC."

"Well, like I said, feel free."

Jen handed him his beer, and Brice took a deep draw. This was the best he'd felt in months. A beautiful woman who had eyes only for him, a great piano, the music flowing from his fingers. Vader on its way to being a real deal. Life was damn good.

What would tonight bring?

9
———

JEN HAD PURPOSELY DAWDLED OVER FINISHING HER WINE while they listened to RJ play in the Boulderado's lobby. She only had one glass, as she was driving, but drew it out as long as she dared.

Brice's stomach's grumbled loud enough for everyone in the lobby to hear. She knew she needed to feed the man, but dithered — uncommon for her— over the decision to cook dinner or eat here. Her body wanted to be home and see where the night would lead.

Her brain told her that was simply insane.

Could she make her body behave? *Of course you can, you're not a teenager, held hostage by hormones.*

Right.

In the end, Brice decided for her by saying three simple words. *Pasta sounds good.*

So they were in her kitchen, making dinner.

Scratch that. She was making dinner and Brice was watching. Not a bad combo as he'd already said the dishes were his contribution to the meal. How lovely was that? Cooking relaxed her, dishes didn't. So she cut fresh basil from her indoor garden, pulled handmade pasta, courtesy of Annie, from the freezer and set to work with the food processor.

Brice was good at uncorking and pouring, and picked a perfect red to go with the Pesto.

In minutes the pasta was ready for tasting. Jen forked up a few strands from the bubbling pot and held them out for Brice to taste.

He blew on it, then his lips folded around the fork as he gently sucked the pasta off. Chewing for a moment, he smiled that dangerously wicked smile. "Perfectly al dente."

No so for her body—it was melting in all the right spots.

She grabbed her wine glass and swigged.

"Whoa, woman, I know wine, and this is expensive."

Ignoring the hint of laughter hidden in his words, she put down the glass, drained the pasta, tossed in the pesto, and took it to the table Brice had set.

Blast it all, he'd lit the candles.

And the fireplace. The man was good.

"This is absolutely the best pesto I've had, even beats Italy," he said after several bites.

"Why, thank you, kind sir. In college Annie and I had an Italian roommate. She would take us to the dorm kitchen late at night and teach us how to not only make sauces, but also the pasta. Annie likes the pasta making, and she's a whiz at Alfredo sauce. We have that every Christmas without fail."

"Except for this year. This year it was a hotel version. Just not the same is it?"

Jen kept her eyes on her plate, stunned he remembered what she was eating that night four days ago and that he was astute enough to realize now why she had been so melancholy.

And you were rude. Rude!

"Why were you in the hotel? Stalking me?" she said with a smile to soften her question.

This time he gulped the wine, then grinned when she raised her brow. "I knew where you were staying—easy to ask the General's secretary. And I wanted to see you. Our last meeting wasn't really a friendly parting—"

"Yeah, being on the losing side of a case is never fun."

"Exactly. And since I'd chosen you to beta test and knew you might refuse once you realized your partner was me, I decided it would be wise to let you know ahead of time. Give you time to sleep on it. I didn't want to disappoint the general by having you refuse him."

"Were you going to tell me about Vader that night?" She asked, intrigued that he cared enough about the general to avoid springing a bad surprise on him.

"Yes, but then when I saw you—"

"I was—"

"You were in full Madame Ice Queen mode."

～

BRICE SAW THE CHANGE IN HER IMMEDIATELY. SHE SAT A BIT straighter, her eyes lost their soft luminance and her gaze sharpened. Crap.

"It's a good facade, Jen, but I know that's not really you, at least not outside work," he risked. "And the fact that you teach for free, offer help when it's needed, even when you don't want to, your stand-off veneer just doesn't work anymore for me."

"This is work. I'm getting paid a great deal of money to test Vader, and I don't want to compromise my findings by falling for the guy who designed it."

Falling for? Did she really say that? He hid his grin, knowing it would only drive her deeper into the very mode he disliked with a passion. Jennifer Malone's reputation was sterling. She didn't have to use that cold pretense.

Everyone one who had any creds in the digital forensic world knew of her and her handpicked team.

And while he'd seen Todd in action during the expert phase of the trial, he got to see him work in the ForceOne office and was intrigued by the eccentricity of the man and his attention to detail.

Then there was striking Susan. Also eccentric; however, they were both brilliant. So Jen didn't need to keep up the pretense of being a cold, shrewd fish.

"So you learned to make pesto in college, what else did you learn?" he asked, trying to get them back to a more personal level.

Leaning back in her chair, she stared at him with a level gaze that didn't bode well.

"That a majority of men are afraid of smart women.

That real friends are hard to come by. That a parent's divorce can wound. That they didn't stay together for the child's sake, and even after they split up, I was simply another bone between them. And lastly I learned to be independent."

Whoa, okay, that explained her withdrawal whenever the subject of divorce came up. And wasn't he just covered with the damned "D" letter? Maybe not as scandalous as the ancient scarlet letter "A," but in Jen's world, he imagined D was just as bad.

"All that on top of learning all the core curriculum," he said, making his voice droll.

"Yep."

He waited, hoping she would ask about his academy life. Then he realized she hadn't thawed yet, so he plunged ahead, hoping a bit of personal reveal would work. If she said "falling for," then there was a bit of desire inside her. He just had to find the way to unlock more.

"At the Academy, I learned how to lead a group of soldiers, to command, even though at first I was terrified I would make a tragic mistake. I learned how to accept orders even if I disagreed with them. And how recalling family moments made it bearable when I was lonely or wondering if I was cut out for that life. I played the piano since I was a child, and sometimes I'd go to the Officer's club and play until I got my bearings back. It didn't matter that the club was empty, it mattered that I played."

He watched Jen steadily, the pesto growing cold between them. She'd turned on the sad little Christmas tree when they'd arrived home, and he worked the fire and added the candles. The room was warmly lit, and he wanted that same sense in her eyes.

Slowly they lost their icy edge. That was close. Let the world see Madame Ice Queen, he wanted the Jennifer Malone who was fascinating, funny, loyal, and a fine cook to boot.

"You play like a pro."

"Mom was a tough taskmaster. We lived in a small town in central Kansas where Dad ran the hardware, farm, and department store all lumped together in a huge old barn next to our house. The town grew up around the Young homestead, so Dad's commute was really about a hundred yards, across the driveway and back. Elementary school and junior high schools were in town , but when they changed the junior high to a middle school, they moved it to the next town over, where Caro went to middle school, and I went to high school right next door. I drove, she took the bus."

"If the schools were next to each other, why did she take the bus? Were you a horrible driver or something else?"

JEN SIPPED HER WINE AS SHE WAITED FOR BRICE'S ANSWER. Was he a horrible driver? That would be awful.

She loved to drive, and when she had the opportunity, pushed the speed limit, just to feel the exhilaration of what the BMW could do.

Brice had that gleam in his eyes, as if he were about to reveal a major joke.

"Caro would laugh her head off hearing you ask if I were horrible. To her, yes. I was too cautious for her."

Jen's laughter came straight from her heart. Darn the man, he was just too much fun to be around.

"You know the movie *Footloose*?" Brice asked.

She nodded. "Yes, I love it. The music, Kevin Bacon, John Lithgow."

"Well, Caro was Ariel, not quite as wild, but close."

Brice closed his eyes for a second, a frown wrinkling his brow, and she wondered if he were remembering some difficult incident.

"People think she's a hellraiser," he recited with a slightly hick, movie-perfect accent. "Is she?" came Kevin Bacon's line in faultless mimicry. "I think she's been kissed a lot," again in that country hick accent.

Jen laughed so hard, tears leaked down her cheeks. "Oh, my God, do you know all the lines?"

"No, they stick in my head when it relates to something in my life. It's a gift."

"That it is. Let me get some more warm pasta. Top off the wine, will you?"

Jen brought back new bowls filled with hot pesto, and for a few moments neither of them talked, as it would have been quite rude to talk with one's mouth full of green food.

Finally they both slowed down.

"Have you been?"

"What?"

"Kissed a lot?"

The wine went down the wrong way, and Jen struggled to keep from choking. When she could finally catch her breath, she wondered about her answer. "Well, I'm not in high school anymore, so yes, I have been. I like kissing. But the times when my toes curled because of a kiss, I could count on both hands and still have six fingers left."

10

Now Brice had a new goal in life. To make Jen's toes curl.

And he wanted to start right now, this very minute.

Her fingers caressed the bowl of the wine glass up and down, and a groan nearly passed his lips. Instead he quickly forked up the last of his pesto and swallowed without chewing.

"Done?" She asked.

Undone, you mean. "Yep, it was the best pesto that's ever crossed my lips."

"Coffee by the fire?"

Wicked woman. "Sure, but let me help you clear the table."

Their movements in the kitchen were precise and fast, as if they both couldn't wait to get to the couch by the fire.

As Jen made the coffee, he grabbed the candles off the dining table and put them on the coffee table. Then, on a total whim, he grabbed the huge pillows on the couch along with the Christmas-themed throw and set up a nest on the rug in front of the fire.

Pleased with his plan, he heard the tap, tap, tap of Jen's boots against the wood floor and experienced a moment of indecision. Hell, he could command a force of cyber geeks around the world, even command combat, but staging this battle had him second guessing everything.

"Nice, I haven't done this for quite a while." She put the cups on the table behind them and sank to her knees, propped up one of the cushions against the table and leaned back against it.

"Oh, and you do this with your dates?"

"Never done this with a date, and you, retired Major Brice Young, are not a date, so my record is still intact." She grabbed her cup and took a sip.

Ouch. He wondered if any of her dates ever got to sleep over. Or if they had to leave before sleep set in?

That thought pained him more than Jen's considering her record still safe. Waking up with this woman next to him, her long blonde hair tousled on the pillows, long lean legs entwined with his, would be a great way to spend the rest of his mornings.

Suddenly his dense brain realized that Jen was beginning to mean a lot more to him than his vow of breaking her hated moniker. She was just about everything he could possibly want in a mate. And mate to him meant marriage. He couldn't get the Kansas out of him and just settle for a living arrangement. Corny, but true.

"Jennifer Malone, what do you want from life? A dog,

kids, marriage, not necessarily in that order? Travel, a ski chalet in Switzerland?"

That made her laugh and lightened his own mood as well. He settled down on the cushions, stretching out until his toes nearly touched the fire, and laced his fingers behind his head. He hoped she'd take him seriously and answer.

"What, you're not going to also ask about my astrological sign?"

JEN HADN'T MEANT TO ASK THAT QUESTION, IT JUST CAME out as a defensive play. A flippant remark to release some of the tension she'd felt seeing the nest he'd created on the floor. Intimate, lovely and something she could get used to.

Way too easily.

"Aries. It fits you," he said in a near whisper.

Okay, not surprising that he knew her sign. They both had the ability to find on the computer nearly anything on anybody if they wanted to.

"I don't think two Aries go well together," she said.

"Touché, you checked as well. But you're wrong about not working well together."

"I said go well—"

"I know, and I'm going to prove you wrong. And now that we're done with the pickup lines, I really want to know what your life dreams are."

Brice took the cup from her nearly nerveless fingers and placed it with his on the low table behind them. In the flickering fire light, he traced her lips with his fingers, then gently cupped her face while she stayed absolutely still.

Her mind, on the other hand, raced back to the thought of his nimble fingers playing the piano, and what they could do to her. Hot flames began to burn in her lower body.

Jen closed her eyes, thinking it would ground her, then realized she didn't want to be grounded. She opened them to his intent gaze.

He was waiting for her to make the next move. Giving her the right of refusal.

Other than that moment in the restaurant high above DC when he'd wiped that droplet wine from her lips, this was the closest they'd been.

And now, bathed with only the firelight and the candles, Brice only inches away, she felt a flutter of panic.

This was wrong. The wrong time, the wrong man.

No, not the wrong man, but the circumstances were wrong.

She should simply pull away and become the hated Madame Ice Queen for the rest of the week.

She should, but as she studied the shadowed, angular planes of his face, the question and desire in his gray eyes combined with the hint of promise on his lips, Jen argued that this was a short-term fling. Brice was leaving as soon as the beta testing was done, a couple more days at most.

But you don't like short-term flings. You want it all, the happily ever after, forever.

But I might like this one.

She touched his lips with her finger, then ran her hand

around his cheek to his neck, feeling the crisp thick hair that touched the collar of his shirt.

Pulling his face closer, her lips touched his, accepting this moment with him. The answers about her life dreams were for another time, another man.

Not for a short-term fling with divorced, retired Major Brice Young.

BRICE HATED THE HESITATION AND DOUBT IN JEN'S EYES before her lips claimed his. After his divorce and until now, he'd allowed the passionate side of his nature to come out through playing the piano. Either at his favorite bar, where they fondly nicknamed him Piano Man, or at the Andrews officers club.

Passion shouldn't have to be thought about, it should happen. The thinking part was before it started. He'd put the cushions on the floor and she'd accepted. Still, he gave her the choice, would always give her the choice to go to the next step. Nevertheless, he'd hoped her answer would be yes.

Remembering the softness of Jen's lips since Christmas was perhaps unmanly, but that moment had fired all sorts of uncomfortable dreams of her beside him, beneath him, hovering over him, snuggling against him.

Right now, he'd take the kiss Jen offered and work on the other stuff during the rest of the week.

She nipped at his lower lip and sucked it as if in

retaliation for that moment in DC. Then she settled her mouth over his.

His hand moved from her face to the back of her head, bringing her closer. As if she knew what he'd been thinking, she moved her body so it lay against him.

Oh, sweet God. Then she canted one hip over his, still not breaking their kiss.

Holding her tight, he shifted their positions so she was beneath him. Coming up for needed air, he watched Jen studying him, her gaze soft but searching.

Her hair was tousled, tendrils framing her face, and her lips slightly swollen, on the way to being well loved.

She wrapped one leg over his, bringing them as close as possible with clothing still on.

Spurred on by her move, he risked running a hand down the curves of her body to her hip and back up, cupping one breast, earning a ragged gasp.

Heaven.

In retaliation, Jen opened the top couple of buttons on his shirt and slipped her hand inside, running fingers lightly, tantalizingly across his chest. Then she opened the rest of the buttons, pulled the shirt from his jeans, and ran a hot trail of kisses from his collar bone to the belt of his pants.

"God, woman, stop."

"Really?"

"Yes. No. Yes." He groaned as she cupped him.

He fumbled with the small buttons on her silk shirt, and as he glanced up to her face, a smile hovered on her lips and laughter teased her eyes. But she didn't offer to help him.

Finally he was rewarded with a nude-colored lace bra barely covering her breasts. And hot damn if it didn't hook in front. He released the clasp and the bra fell away. His own breath grew ragged. Smooth ivory skin reflected the flickering golden firelight.

Brice wanted to savor this moment and make her squirm at the same time. Moving onto his side gave him the opportunity to caress one breast, circle the rosy nipple with his finger, and follow it with his tongue.

Then he paid homage to her other breast.

Jen's eyes were closed, his sleeve fisted in her hand. Small exquisite pants escaped from her parted lips.

He touched the apex of her jean-clad thighs, earning a groan.

Brice wanted her writhing beneath him, without the barriers now separating them. He wanted Jennifer Malone, not only for tonight but for all the nights to come.

And knew if they made love this night, those other nights wouldn't happen.

She'd come to her senses, and it would be back to Major Brice Young, retired, and Jennifer Malone, Madame Ice Queen.

So he stopped.

Which was the hardest thing he'd ever done.

But hopefully forgoing making her his right now would be worth the pain. "If we're going to run that long Vader attack tomorrow and go snowshoeing, I better get the dishes done and hit the sack."

Her eyes regained their focus, and she started to move as if embarrassed by her state of undress.

Brice couldn't let it end like this. Before she could move or say a word, he covered her lips once again. "I want you, Jennifer Malone, make no mistake about my need for you. But after Vader, when we're free of the working relationship, we can come together without doubts or regrets."

She allowed him to clasp her bra, then swatted his hand away and buttoned her own shirt. He didn't bother straightening his own. Getting untangled from her and the pillows, he finally grabbed their coffee cups.

Jen made a move to get up. "No, stay there, it's way more comfortable," he said.

And left her.

When he poked his head into the room a few minutes later, the couch pillows were back in place, the fireplace and candles dark, and she'd left.

He wondered what tomorrow would bring.

11

Oddly Jen wasn't mad at Brice for last night, but she had given herself a good talking to before she went to bed, aching from unreleased passion.

This morning, feeling more in control, she slipped on her snow gear of silk long johns, black stretch pants and a turtle neck, then went downstairs to greet the day and the man who'd melted her into a puddle of lust last night.

She was old enough not to be embarrassed over the evening's passionate moment but still paused before she entered the kitchen, hoping it wouldn't be uncomfortable between them today.

Jen enjoyed Brice's company, and his body, well, it was purely magnificent. He stayed in shape and it showed.

Stop those thoughts, or you'll melt again.

Maybe she should nix the idea of snowshoeing. Alone with him for hours in the car and on the trails would be a form of torture—could she handle it? She wasn't really a wilderness child any longer, and she could use that as an excuse to not go on this excursion.

How about no excuses, Jen? You're in your thirties and don't need excuses. Just say you've rethought the idea and it's a bad one.

She stepped into the kitchen to find it empty, though she should have guessed. There wasn't the scent of fresh coffee being brewed, and Brice seemed to need a cup to wake up just as she did.

Jen's cell phone rang with Annie's ringtone of *When You Wish Upon A Star*, and her picture popped up on the screen.

A smile and a sense of calm spread through Jen.

"You up? I see lights on," Annie said.

"Yeah, where are you?"

"Front door."

"Why didn't you ring the bell?"

"I didn't know if maybe you and Brice—"

"Nope," Jen said as she opened the door.

Two pairs of snowshoes and poles were piled on the porch and Annie held a baggie of her cookies.

"Damn."

Annie pulled back with a puzzled expression. "What? I thought you wanted to go on this trek? At least that's what your text indicated last night."

Jen yanked her into the house, leaving the pile at the door. "I'm so glad to see you."

"Uh-oh, what happened with Brice?" Annie said, making her own cup of coffee in the kitchen. "You didn't sleep with him, did you?"

"Not yet."

She laughed, making Jen blush. "Shades of our conversation a few weeks ago, but then it was Cole who was the subject of that question."

"Yeah, and I told you to quit worrying or some such nonsense."

"So take your own advice."

"You know it's more complicated than that."

"As was my issue. But being honest worked it out, thankfully."

"Brice is a job."

Annie let loose another bright peal of laughter. "That makes you sound like you're in a less than honorable profession."

Jen shook her head. "Be serious, this is trouble. The man is amazing in so many ways, but he's divorced, and he's basically living out of a suitcase."

"Yeah, so he's in transition."

Jen placed hands on hips and gave Annie her best get-real look.

"Okay, so you have an issue with commitment, rightfully so, Your parents sucked at both marriage and being parents. And you're afraid that the apple, being you, doesn't fall far from the tree."

"Hey, I have the dating record to prove it."

"You're picky, and that's great, but Jen, just maybe you're pushing men away because you think your relationship will be just like your parents', sour and ending in divorce. Daddy taught you how to love and be loved, to accept that gift, something your folks could never manage. They were wrong for each other, didn't try to make it work for your sake, and then basically forgot about you in their disappointment with life and each other."

"Okay, maybe I can swallow all that. Maybe. But I don't want to risk a marriage and maybe have kids that will be hurt if the relationship goes south."

Annie gave her a hug. "You were really burned, but if you're serious at all about Brice now or in a few days," she winked at Jen, "put everything on the table. His answers may be the death knell to the relationship, but it's better to know up front. Right?"

Annie waited and Jen couldn't answer her.

"Oh, Jen. You're past the too deep stage? You've never, ever fallen this fast, this hard."

"I know," Jen said, trying to keep the keening wail out of her voice.

Just then the back door opened and in walked the subject of their conversation.

Jen and Annie looked at each other, then back, at the knowing smile gracing Brice's lips. "My ears are on fire."

Annie grinned in response. "Snowshoeing equipment is out front. I brought a cap and an extra pair of gloves for you, courtesy of Cole."

She slid off the kitchen stool and pecked Jen on the cheek. "On the table, soon," she whispered and left.

"Nice of Annie to bring the equipment. Now you can't back out on me," Brice said.

"I wasn't going to back out, whatever gave you that idea?"

"Male intuition."

"I didn't know males had that trait."

"Sometimes intuition is handed to us, like when a lady escapes a comfy nest by the fire and removes all traces of a lovely evening."

"You're the one that left—"

"Jen, I had to recover my sanity. I want this to work. You can't deny there's chemistry between us."

She was nailed by the earnestness in his eyes, the intensity of his posture. He wasn't joking or feeding her a line.

"Getting up and leaving you was nearly the hardest thing I've done in a long, long time," he said, voice low.

Then, thankfully, he turned away to make a cup of coffee, because while he didn't say he loved her, each word he'd uttered vibrated with intensity. Something that had never happened to her before. Her face flamed, and her breath quickened.

*Put everything on the table...you've never fallen this deep this fast...*Annie's words played back in her mind. As did her answer. Jen needed to finish up the job of vetting Vader, and then she'd take that risk and see where she landed.

"I've got Vader's attack ready to launch, and unless there's something you need at the office, I can go ahead, send it off, and we can start our adventure,"

Jen pulled herself together. "Nope, nothing at the office I need."

"By the way, I was poking around in the lab last night and found the duplicate of your coffee machine in a cupboard, even half and half in the fridge—"

"Ewww, it's expired. I hope you didn't drink it."

"No, I didn't need coffee last night. But why the lab and all the important accoutrements there? It's less than fifty yards to the house to get whatever you need."

"Ever worked 'round the clock or just didn't want to let go of a new idea even for a few minutes, afraid you'll forget something?"

He nodded.

"Also I didn't want it in the house, because I decided ForceOne work needed to be separate from my life."

His head shake was slight, but the minute she saw it, she realized she'd said it again, keeping life and work separate.

This time she didn't mean him.

Jen was a woman after his own heart: nothing got in the way of a project. Something his 'ex' couldn't understand. It was part of his upbringing—you worked until the work was done. At times it was a ball and chain, and during the building of Vader's algorithms, there were times when Brice had to walk away for a short while. But after his mind was clear, he attacked the problem again, and the solution usually appeared in the mess of equations on the paper.

Bethany simply walked away from her problems and let someone clean them up. Thank God he was no longer the somebody.

But Brice didn't like the way Jen kept bringing up work

and life, working so hard to keep them separate. Sometimes the lines blurred.

He set up his laptop on the travertine counter, booted it up and launched his most advanced attack yet. The "low and slow" would take at least twenty-four hours of trying a variety of malicious attacks and differing patterns.

"Okay, we're done. Rocky Mountain National Park, here we come," Brice said. He followed Jen out of the kitchen, grabbed the gear Annie had left on the porch and headed for the garage.

"I'm feeling a little bit guilty about taking this time off, considering what General Cartwright is paying me." Jen threw her own boots and warm snow clothes on top of the gear Brice put into the back of her BMW.

"Why? It's a long attack and all we'd be doing is twiddling our thumbs if we didn't have this adventure. Unless, of course, you'd like to avoid me today," he said, settling into the seat next to her, and giving her a Cheshire grin.

Jen just raised a brow and backed out of the driveway.

There wasn't much more testing to be done to prove Vader was thoroughly vetted and their work finished. Then came the real job of convincing Jen he didn't carry the plague. As much as Vader meant to him and his future, a future with her was beginning to carry equal importance, maybe more.

Jen headed out US 36 along the foothills, through Lyons and up the canyon. Brice let the impossibly white and glittery blanket of snow on the ground, rocks, and trees act as a balm to his soul. Jen was a fast yet excellent driver, and the BMW was an awesome machine.

At her invitation, he looked at the playlists on her iPod and picked Beethoven's Seventh Symphony, adding another layer to the nearly perfect morning.

It could only have been better had she woken up beside him.

He paid the park's entrance fee, and they headed up to Bear Lake. Falling in line behind a long procession of vehicles, they slowly climbed the final few super-twisty miles to a nearly full parking lot

"This I didn't expect. Where did all these people come from?" he asked, a bit disappointed as he'd hoped for a private adventure with Jen.

"School is out, or people take the week off between Christmas and New Year's. And if it's a clear day like this after a snow fall ... well, it's Colorado outdoor time."

She parked the car and pulled a large canvas bag to the front seat, handing him the thermos to hold while she rummaged through the bag to find something.

"What did you put in the thermos?"

"Hot cocoa."

"God, you are perfect."

"Just wait until you see my form using snowshoes and you'll change your mind. Here they are. Annie brought some of her cookies when she dropped off the gear." Jen held up the bag. "Hungry?"

For you. "Nope, I'll wait until we're done, then I'm sure I'll be starving. Altitude does that, you know."

They bundled up and carried their snowshoes and poles to the beginning of the trail.

Even though it had snowed last night, a path had already been started around the lake. Good thing, because fresh snow, while beautiful, was a lot harder to work through.

"Okay, remember how to do this?" she asked.

"We'll see." He just prayed he didn't fall flat on his face with the first foot plant.

Twenty yards later and he still hadn't fallen. Jen stayed behind him, making sure he got the hang of it. "Wow, I think I actually remember how to snowshoe. Want to go ahead now?"

"Sure. You're very pokey," she said with a grin.

JEN STAYED IN THE TRACKS ALREADY FORGED AND GOT QUITE a rhythm going; plant left pole, pick up right foot, then repeat on the other side.

She wore black stretch pants over silk long johns and a black down parka that fell below her hips, belted tightly against the cold. A black knit cap covered her head, and wrapped around her neck was her favorite magenta muffler for added warmth.

Wanting to make a great impression, Jen moved as fast as she could through the cold and thigh-deep snow that threatened to sink her with every step. Looking over her shoulder, Brice impressed her the way he was keeping up, even if he huffed and puffed. Heck, coming from DC's sea level to this altitude would do a number on anyone, including her, and she lived at a mile high plus. Bear Lake was another three thousand feet higher. But no way would she stop now. Halfway round, she'd take pity on him and stop. And hope she wouldn't collapse.

In a few more minutes, they were only yards behind the family of four that started off way before them.

The little girl had moved to the side of the path, looking thoroughly miserable. She simply stood there, her little nose running and tears about to fall and freeze on her cheeks. Her mom turned around to check on her. "Come on, sweetie, we'll stop at the big rock just up ahead, and you can warm up with a cup of soup," she called to her.

Jen's heart went right out to the sad child. It could have been her at that age, except she had never been called sweetie. But she'd had to do things she hadn't wanted to do just like this little one.

Jen stopped beside her. "Hey, I'm Jen and this is Brice. If you want, we can get there together, okay?"

The little girl started to trudge forward. Jen stayed right beside her, forging a new path through the deep snow. It was harder work, but the little girl seemed a bit less upset.

"That's Daddy's new girlfriend. She calls me sweetie. My name is Cindy."

Jen had to curb her smile, for it was obvious by the way she emphasized her name, Cindy didn't like being called "sweetie."

They had nearly caught up with Daddy and the girlfriend when the path narrowed around a series of large boulders. Jen waited for Cindy to go first and then stepped into the path.

Her snowshoe caught on something, and she couldn't plant her pole fast enough to keep from falling.

She went down sideways, just missing a boulder with her head. The snowshoe remained caught and her ankle twisted.

12

———

Brice saw Jen's fall in slow motion and felt stuck in tar as he tried to move fast enough to catch her.

Missed her by a foot.

With the snow half burying her, she struggled to reach her left ankle. He released the binding on her snowshoes, reached under her arms and lifted her out of the snow cocoon.

He noticed she hung onto him and didn't put any weight on that foot.

"How bad is it?" He put an arm around her to balance her better and began to brush off the snow around her hat and neck.

"Hurts like hell, but I'm sure I didn't break anything."

"Okay, how would you know that?"

"I broke my arm in junior high and Doc set it. I know broken."

"Then I'll take your word for it, Doctor Malone."

That got a weak smile out of her.

"Daddy, Daddy, come quick," Cindy called in her high little voice.

"No, Cindy, I'm okay," Jen said.

Brice bit down his laughter at Cindy's stubborn look.

"Daddy can help."

Brice brushed the last of the snow from Jen's collar, then checked her over. Her lips were pinched closed, obviously against the pain. He glanced at Cindy, who was looking up the trail for her daddy, so he quickly bussed Jen's lips. Then again as they softened beneath his.

He'd been worried that after last night she'd go into a full-on return of her chilly nickname. And while she'd been a bit distant, she hadn't been cold or aloof. So he'd at least melted one layer of her facade.

Jen leaned against him, and it was killing him that she hurt. "You're going to be okay, I'll get you back to the car." He was prepared to either sling her over his shoulder cave-man style or have her ride piggyback to get her to the car, but she was going to get back safely and then they'd head to her doctor's. Just in case something was indeed broken.

"I'm glad you're here, Brice. Stupid of me to fall."

"Not stupid, just an accident. You're sure you didn't hit your head?"

"Why?"

"Because you said you were glad I was here," he finished with a grin and got a wan one in return.

Cindy's dad and girlfriend reached them.

"Daddy's a paramedic," Cindy said, pride lacing each word.

"I think it twisted when I fell."

"She fell helping me," the little girl said morosely.

"Sweetie, you were doing fine," the girlfriend said. "If you needed help—"

"It wasn't her fault at all, and she was a trooper moving up the path. Not. Her. Fault." Jen's tone brooked no argument, and the girlfriend shut up.

"Okay, let's get your boot off, and then we'll get you back to the parking lot. I'm Hank, by the way, and my daughter is correct. I'm a paramedic in Louisville."

Brice cleared the snow off the smallest boulder, and Jen sat on its edge. Hank got her boot off, and Brice winced right along with Jen.

He pulled off the sock and sure enough, her ankle was beginning to swell.

Hank put her sock back on. "Okay, I'm going to pack a bit of snow around it to help the swelling, no boot, and we're going to walk you back."

He looked at Brice who nodded.

Even though he'd have liked to carry her, this was better for her.

JEN FELT LIKE A TOTAL FOOL. ACCIDENTS HAPPENED AS BRICE said, but this was ridiculous.

She now had her snowshoe only on her right foot, her left knee bent so her foot bore no weight, and her arms around Hank and Brice, who basically carried her back to the car, step by slow step. They each held a pole in their outer arm to balance them.

Cindy and the girlfriend followed, carrying the rest of Jen's gear.

Other people on the path had to step aside for the wide trio to get past.

Stupid and embarrassing.

They got to the paved trail entrance, which was mostly cleared of snow, and had to take off their gear.

"I'll get the car," Brice said, holding out his hand for the key. With a reassuring smile for her, he sprinted down the row of vehicles in the over-crowded parking lot.

It took all of Jen's will power to not shout out "be careful" as he slid once on the icy pavement.

A few minutes later, he pulled up to the curb, and Hank helped Jen get into the car, took off her sock and wrung it out. "See your doc—you may have torn a ligament," he advised and handed them his card.

Cindy came up. "I'm sorry."

Jen cupped her cold cheek. "Cindy, it wasn't your fault, and I want you to stop thinking it was. Promise me that, okay?"

The little girl nodded and finally a smile curved her lips.

Hank closed the car door, and Brice drove off after giving them all a wave.

Jen couldn't stop her shivers. "I'm sorry. This kind of ruined the day."

He pulled over to the last bit of paved shoulder in the parking lot and let the vehicle idle. "Hey, the only thing I'm worried about is your ankle. We wanted an adventure, and we got it," he said with a light tone.

It helped immeasurably that he wasn't mad or disappointed that his day was ruined. Jen had witnessed her father become furious at her mom when she'd been in a car accident. It hadn't been her fault, but her dad screamed and swore. Then he apologized, saying he'd just been worried.

Reaching into the backseat, Brice grabbed the canvas bag Jen had packed and pulled out the thermos and two cups.

"Let me, I'm not helpless," she said, cross that her voice was still sounded a bit wavery.

Jen poured two cups of hot cocoa half full and handed him a cookie as well.

The man beside her was a rock, someone she knew she could depend on and who put her welfare first. He was everything she'd ever wished for in a partner.

Except she just couldn't rid herself of the fear that he'd chosen badly once and divorced, and that it could happen again. She wanted forever once she chose to marry. Relationships took work and compromise, not anger, accusations, then finally divorce.

Tears gathered for what might have been. Jen closed her eyes and leaned her head against the headrest, hoping none of the tears escaped.

∼

BRICE KEPT GLANCING AT JEN, WHO HAD RECLINED THE SEAT and closed her eyes.

They rode in silence for miles, and though he wanted

to say something, anything, he didn't want to wake her if she was asleep.

"You know, it's going to take us hours to get back if you keep driving at this pace," she said.

"New car, snow and a snake for a road. Give me time to get used to it, Little Miss Impatient."

That earned him a small grin, even if her eyes remained shut.

"What hospital or urgent care do you want to go to?"

"None. Ice and elevation, plus some aspirin will do the trick. I even have crutches at home if I need them."

He took the last sharp curve and headed down the straighter part of the park's road, picking up speed. "Why on earth would you have something like crutches around?"

"Just a tad bit clumsy. Twisted the same ankle last spring when I was doing some gardening. I was supposed to go to rehab but didn't make the time. So it's weaker. Guess I learned my lesson, eh?"

What could he say to that? He was worried about the pain she was so obviously experiencing as another grimace tightened her lips.

"I'm guessing you don't have aspirin in this swanky car."

A slight shake of her head.

"Then why don't I stop at that market we passed on the way into town, and I'll run in and get some. Might as well start easing that pain now."

Jen opened her eyes, rolled her head sideways and gave him a beaming smile that so mesmerized him he nearly missed the next curve.

"That would be lovely. Thank you for thinking about it."

"Wouldn't anybody when someone they cared about hurt?" God, did that just pop out of his mouth? And while it was true, Jen didn't need to hear it from him until after this beta testing was done and they could be on a different footing. Which he hoped was tomorrow.

"One would think, but Annie and Doc were the only two people in my life that ever looked out for me."

"Tell me about Doc. He sounds like a wonderful man."

"Was. He died several years ago. I'd love to tell you about him, because he was the most important man in my life. From about kindergarten age, I learned to make a bowl of cereal as it was often the only kind of meal I'd have. I'm not telling you this to make you feel sorry for me, but because I've never loved anyone like Annie and Doc."

Brice wanted to grab her up and hold her, make her feel like she could love him, too. "So where was this, Maine?"

"Yes, you remembered! A small community, inland. The whole town knew I was the poster child for latch-key kid. Mrs. Barton, who owned the bakery, gave me cookies or a cupcake when I'd walk by on my way home from school. And Andy, who worked at the hardware store, a place kind of like what your dad owned, would make sure I had a jacket, gloves, whatever.

"Then one day Doc came by Dad's trailer because Annie told him I wasn't at school and might be sick. My parents were divorced by this time, and I was staying with Dad. He was in Bangor for ten of the fourteen days I was with him. If Doc hadn't come, I would have died. I was scared and too sick to do anything but cry with the high fever. I had the 'flu. From that moment on, the Hamiltons were my family.

"Doc was the only doctor for a huge region and was often gone on calls. When she wasn't in school, Annie would go with him. And when I joined the family, I'd go along, too. He couldn't adopt me of course, so I wasn't able to be with them all the time until I turned eighteen, but when I could get away, the only place I wanted to be was right there with them. I miss the man with every fiber of my being."

Did he dare ask her about her folks? What the hell, the in for a penny thing. "And your folks?"

Jen wrinkled her nose.

"It was while I was in fourth grade. That's when they got smart and divorced. Two weeks with Dad, then four weeks with Mom. I was a bone they used to fight over for more money. Never more time. I don't hear from them, and I don't care if I ever hear from them."

He finally understood just how much her parents had scarred her. They hadn't wanted her and their marriage was a farce. She'd had no experience with folks who had a good marriage.

And worse, apparently to Jen, divorce simply seemed a way to avoid responsibility.

13

JEN GLANCED AT BRICE AFTER HER OUTBURST ABOUT HER parents and didn't see censure or disapproval. But then he was also a member of the same not-so-exclusive club.

And since the door to revealing her life was open, she figured it was the perfect time to take Annie's advice and start seeing just how much they had or didn't have in common.

"Brice, do you want kids if you ever get married again?" *Why, of all the questions you could have asked was this the one to start off with?*

And her timing was off, as he'd just pulled into the market's parking lot.

Or maybe it was perfect as he could escape the loaded question.

Jen realized she didn't want him to escape the question. *God, woman, are you daft or what? Why do you think he's the 'one'?*

Because he's funny, smart, and way too handsome not to be snapped up again. One more reason, a big one in her experience with men—he wasn't intimidated by her in the least. Not like most of her dates. Not like Frederick.

Thank God I never fell hard for that man. Sure it had stung to hear him say that he couldn't feel on equal footing with her, but he was nothing like Brice, who liked her mind.

She didn't think of herself as above anyone, but she couldn't pretend to be something she wasn't. She didn't want to hide her mind.

Brice didn't ever make her feel that she couldn't simply be Jennifer Malone with her degrees attached, let alone creator of ForceOne, tops in its field. They were part and parcel of who she was.

"Why are you asking? Because of Cindy? Because you don't want them? Or because you do?" Brice signaled to turn into a row of parking spaces.

Wow, what a great way to turn the tables.

"You first, after all, I asked the question. And yes, Cindy wasn't happy and obviously disliked her dad's new girlfriend. It made me think about it."

"And that surprises you? Kids rarely take to a usurper. We don't even know how long the girlfriend has been in the picture. This could be a first family outing, and then for sure Cindy isn't going to like her. Maybe it wasn't because of divorce, maybe Cindy's mom died."

"Granted. But still…" Now she wanted nothing more than to retract the question. Not because she didn't want to know, she did, but what Brice said was true. All she saw was a sad little girl and a daddy who had a girlfriend. She'd put herself into Cindy's shoes and then assumed the worst because that's what Jen herself had experienced.

Annie would think her the biggest ninny but would temper her scolding with a hug. Brice might be entirely put off, and honestly she couldn't blame him.

He pulled into a spot but left the motor running. "When Bethany told me she was pregnant, my first reaction was disbelief. We'd only been together a short while. But the only honorable thing I could do was propose. And shortly afterward we had the full military wedding. It was all so whirlwind. Then, before I could fully wrap my head around all the changes in my life, she miscarried."

Jen met his gaze full on.

"And I didn't feel anything other than relief, and then guilt about feeling it. It took a few months for me to realize that the relief wasn't about not having a child, it was about not having one with Bethany.

"I know what I'm going to say is considered heresy, but the next realization I had was that I didn't really need children in my life to feel fulfilled. I needed a partner who wasn't depending totally on me to make them fulfilled. I don't have an overwhelming paternal urge, but if my wife got pregnant, I figure I'd be a pretty good dad because I had a great role model. Did my answer kill whatever feelings you might have had for me?"

He cupped her cheek, touched her lips with his finger,

then pulled back and waited for her answer, his gaze never leaving hers.

It didn't unnerve her, it made her feel like her answer was the most important thing in the world to him.

"No." She drew the word out slowly. "Kids were never a part of my adult agenda. You already know about my parents. Annie's mom, who was a divorcee when she married Doc, left them when Annie was young. So I've not had a single good role model. You, however, have, so while I'm surprised, I'm not disappointed."

Practically before the word left her lips, Brice leaned forward and planted a kiss that was filled with such promise she nearly broke her vow of staying away from members of "club divorced."

"So why did you divorce Bethany?"

"Marrying her was a mistake."

God, there it was. Throw away a marriage because you made a mistake, instead of trying to work on it. Divorce was too easy these days. Heck, you could have a hangnail and get a divorce.

"But—"

This time Jen put a finger to his lips for a completely different reason than Brice's against her lips only moments ago.

She didn't want to hear more.

If and when she married, it would be forever. There would be no mistake, no second guessing. No temporary insanity plea.

A deep, invisible gash scored Jen's heart.

They had a few days left to work together, and she'd

pretend everything was fine *and* professional between them. But try as hard as she could, she wasn't able don that once impregnable cloak woven from ice. Madame Ice Queen had been melted.

At great cost.

Jen's finger trembled against Brice's lips. He caught the distance in her gaze before she turned to face forward and folded her hands in her lap.

What had he said that changed her from revealing her heart to the pain he sensed now filled her?

He quickly replayed their conversation.

It wasn't the having kids thing. That seemed to be okay with her.

Jen changed when he'd said he'd made a mistake in marrying Bethany.

He should have chosen a better word, but honestly it had been just as he said.

She hadn't let him explain. He wore the letter D and that was that in her eyes.

His fingers tightened on the steering wheel.

The hell it was. This was going to be a challenge, maybe the biggest of his life, but he'd be damned if she was going to push him out of her life.

And he knew she expected him to be mad or act out. Wasn't going to happen. He didn't have a baby sister for nothing. He knew the right and wrong way to get what he wanted, and he wanted Jen.

Taking a breath and relaxing his fingers, he felt the calm of battle cloak him. "Did you say aspirin was okay or did you want something else?"

"Aspirin will do the trick. Thanks."

He left the car running, made fast tracks into and out of the market, and was back in the BMW in minutes.

Opening the cardboard package and breaking the seal on the bottle, he shook out two tablets into the upturned palm of her hand. What he really wanted to do was kiss it, and then her slim, elegant wrist, all the way up to her lips.

She swallowed them with a topped off cup of hot cocoa and the remaining bite of her cookie.

"Thanks, Brice."

He noticed she'd refilled his cup as well. So she wasn't totally pushing him away.

A good sign?

JEN DIDN'T WANT TO THEIR LAST FEW DAYS TO BE STRAINED, she wanted their partnership to end on a good note. After all Vader was a magnificent tool and Brice should be proud of it. He could take it back to DC and start building his business while she could start healing.

So the few minutes Brice was in the market getting her aspirin, she fought back the ache that filled her. One that had nothing to do with her ankle.

And she'd grasp that excuse for any remaining melancholy Brice might sense in her. For it undeniably hurt. Not as much as her heart, but enough to play the charade.

THE TIGHTNESS AROUND JEN'S MOUTH LOOSENED AS HE drove the BMW down the canyon faster than he thought he could. He was going to get one of these beauts—it had everything he wanted except maybe a convertible top. But someday, if Vader made it as big as he thought it would, he could have both.

"Like the Bimmer, huh?"

Her eyes were open and had lost a degree of their earlier distance he'd so hated. Even while her voice held a note of sadness. For them?

"Love it, it's amazing on the roads. I can't imagine what it would be like on a non-snowy surface."

"Yeah, all we've had since you've been here is snow and more snow."

"It's okay, I like it. Winter here gives you a feeling of warmth, of home and hearth. Not so much in DC." He laughed at himself. "Sorry, but Boulder and Colorado brings out the sappy side." *Not to mention you, Miss Jennifer Malone.*

"I feel the same way about Boulder. Summer makes me want to be outside all the time, to enjoy the intense blue of the clear sky, the crisp mornings and the late afternoon thunderstorms. Winter? It's the time for nesting. Enjoy the snow recreation, or a walk, then come home, wrap yourself up in a blanket by the fire and just be."

"Wow, you have a sappy side as well, don't you?" he said lightly, trying not to lose this tiny bit of the Jen he knew was hiding beneath a world of hurt and distrust.

"I do, and don't you dare tell anyone or I'll tell them you're a liar. Turn here."

He did and moments later parked the SUV in the garage, retrieved the crutches after Jen told him where they were stored, and helped her make her way into the living room.

He started the fire and wrapped the big, thick shawl from the couch around her, tucking her in like a mummy.

"Wine and takeout, okay? Then we'll check on Vader. What's your favorite Chinese?"

Brice called in the order and filled two glasses with pinot grigio, putting another bottle in the fridge to cool.

Her modern house had grown on him. He loved the city and thought once again, if there was to be a woman in his life, it had to be Jennifer Malone.

Back in the living room, *his* woman was asleep in her cocoon. Placing her wine glass on the coffee table, he cradled his and wandered over to the big picture window and stared at a star. It seemed to float down from the heavens and hover on the side of the mountain.

He remembered from his Academy days that the star on Flagstaff Mountain was lit only during the holiday season. He'd seen it once. Tonight it was magical, its light reflecting off the snow beneath it giving it a soft glow. It felt as if the star were shining just for him.

A sense of calm determination filled him, a better way

to approach winning Jen over than the spur of challenge he'd felt earlier.

The doorbell rang and he glanced at his watch. Thirty minutes had passed as he stared at the wondrous star, envisioning a life with the woman who was asleep only feet from him.

Jen stirred as the bell rang again.

14

WHEN THE TAKEOUT ARRIVED, JEN SILENTLY WATCHED BRICE make another nest for them on the floor in front of the fire. She saw him hesitate, and wondered if he was rethinking the intimate nature of the gesture, then shake his head as he moved the pillows apart.

"Do you think it's wise ..." she began only to have him disappear from the living room.

"Yes I do," he said, returning moments later with a couple more pillows off the bed in her guest suite.

She wondered why until he helped her settle against the pillow nest, then gently placed those extra pillows under her leg to elevate it.

"At least for tonight it will be more comfortable than sitting with it propped up on a chair," he said.

Jen expected him to make a comment about actually having a guest room, or for him to suggest that he move in for the duration of their work, but he said nothing.

Swallowing a sigh, she thought how so much had changed in the five days they'd been working together. And then changed again.

After getting her settled, Brice replaced the ice pack on her ankle, and they ate right out of the Chinese takeout cartons, using the chopsticks he found in her kitchen.

He didn't mention Vader or needing to look at the logs, which puzzled her. But since it was a low and slow attack, she assumed it hadn't finished.

Which was fine. For the first time, she didn't want to worry about cyber anything. It had been her go-to escape when life got tough or sticky. Tonight she wanted bed.

And tonight especially, Jen wanted the blankness of a dreamless sleep.

Brice helped her up the stairs, then left her after she said she could undress herself.

She didn't get her wish. Instead she tossed and turned, her sleep fitful, filled with memories of her parents, juxtaposed with dreams of Brice. Loving her, then slipping from her arms.

Finally sleep claimed her in the wee hours of the morning.

When she woke, Jen couldn't believe the clock read 9:15 a.m. Incredibly late for her to be just waking up. She pulled the covers back to check on her ankle, relieved to see it hadn't turned black and blue. And while it was still swollen, aspirin would help her deal with the pain.

Dressing quickly in jeans and a yellow fleece pullover, comfy and easy to work crutches in, Jen hobbled her way to the top of the stairs, figuring she could hop down each one.

She found Brice sitting at the bottom of the stairs, working on his laptop, obviously waiting for her. Had he slept in the house? Or used the key she'd given him? "Good morning, have you been sitting there long?"

He looked up with a small smile. "A couple of hours. Good morning back." Putting aside his laptop, he reached her at the top with a few double steps. "I'm going down in front of you, so if you stumble—"

"We'll both fall in a heap at the bottom?"

"Not exactly, I'll catch you. And I slept on the couch."

She smiled, even though she did her best to squelch it. Today already felt different, and they'd barely said a couple of dozen words. "Mind reading again. You could have used the guest room."

"I could have, but I wouldn't have heard you if you needed something."

Wow.

They got to ForceOne by 10 a.m., late by her standards, though she didn't set a schedule for anyone. Jen made a grand entrance on her crutches. Todd rushed over to her, followed quickly by Susan.

"What happened?" Todd asked.

"Later. I'll tell the tale later, promise."

She could tell Todd wasn't happy with her delay in telling them the story as he gave her a long, questioning stare, then glanced at Brice with the same curious look. Only when she crutched over to her workstation did he move back to his.

Jen glanced at Brice, standing by the window, seemingly lost in thought, hands thrust deep into his jean's pockets.

He had been in a different mood this morning also. His smile was intact, but a little less bright and he wasn't as talkative. Maybe he'd realized that they really had no future and he didn't need to be the charming man with the wicked smile any longer. *No, you know it was you that created the distance.*

Missing their camaraderie already, Jen booted up her lab computer and checked Vader's logs. The system had performed impressively, able to detect every sly attack. Printing out the logs, she signed the bottom with a flourish. "Here are the logs from the last assault. Vader is extremely efficient. I'm very impressed," she said.

Brice took the logs, quickly scanned them, then placed them on top of his computer bag. "Thank you. That's a huge compliment coming from someone who is greatly admired in the cyber world. We've got one last task, then believe it or not, we're done. The general will be pleased with how fast this has gone and how well Vader has performed."

"One? I thought we had a couple more days to go. It's only the twenty-ninth." Brice hadn't said anything last night about leaving this soon. Had she done this with her rant? Her obvious pull back?

Of course you did. Isn't this exactly what you were aiming for?

"—a full packet capture, acting as reverse proxy, okay?"

She focused in time to hear the last of Brice's

instructions. Damned if she wouldn't be the consummate professional until the moment he left. "Sure, that shouldn't take long. Maybe what, four hours?"

"We can draw it out that long if you want."

"Draw it out?"

"It shouldn't take that long, but I have plenty of time. My flight isn't leaving until tomorrow early. Again, courtesy of the Air Force."

BRICE STUDIED JEN'S FACE VERY CAREFULLY AS HE announced his travel plans. She paled, her lips opened as if to say something—something he hoped would be *please don't go yet*, and she white knuckled the back of the chair.

Even if she hadn't spoken the words, her body language told him she wasn't all that keen on his leaving.

Brice saw Susan glance between him and Jen and back to him, as Todd stood by the coffee machine looking confused. Susan took Todd's elbow and moved him toward his workstation, then sat down herself, virtually giving them space.

Jen swallowed, then cleared her voice. Another good sign that maybe she'd miss him while he was gone.

"Well ... I guess we should get started. Then get the logs from this...final attack printed and you're vetted."

Her voice was overbright, and her words tumbled over each other. Damn, even if this showed him she wasn't happy with him leaving, he should have told her in the privacy of her house.

He hadn't planned on returning to DC before New Year's, but while Jen was sleeping this morning, he called the general to tell him Vader was nearly done.

General Cartwright put him on hold, and three minutes later told him there would be a plane available for him tomorrow that would get him back in DC just past noon.

He should have waited to call the general until after the New Year. *Nah, you know you had to do this. Even if you're not an officer any longer, the training is there. And Jennifer Malone, the cyber expert, wouldn't expect you to stay if there wasn't testing to be done.*

But maybe Jennifer Malone, the woman, would've wanted you to stay. After all, I told her I'd planned to spend New Year's here.

I should have waited.

"Jen—"

She fluttered her hand in his direction, cutting him off. "Brice, if we're done, then we're done. The general wanted it fast, we're giving it to him. Boulder will still be here after the New Year."

Ouch. Boulder will still be here. Not Jennifer Malone. *What did you expect?*

Well, this wasn't the place to talk and work it out. They needed neutral ground. He thought quickly. "After we're done, how about a celebratory drink at the Boulderado, and listen to RJ play..." he trailed off at the indecisive look on her face.

"I think that would be ... nice, and we have plenty of time as RJ doesn't usually start until four."

He was sure she'd refuse him.

"Then I have a favor to ask. Do you mind if I borrow your car and run a few errands while you hang out with Vader and do the last logs and notes?" Once again he watched her, this time from the corner of his eyes, and got the reaction he was hoping for. Disappointment.

That at least was a good sign. The small things she's said, the night by the fire, they all led him to believe Jen had feelings for him. And as he had that night, he wanted to give her time. Time to trust her heart and trust him. Time to realize he was a forever kind of guy, with the right woman. And that woman was Jennifer Malone.

His errands were simple. There were two empty office spaces that might work for setting up his business. Neither was on the mall, but that was okay, they were both in Boulder. And even though time was growing short to set up headquarters for his business, he didn't want to tell her he was searching in Boulder. It could force her to make a decision about them, and that was the last thing he wanted. She'd either learn to listen to her heart or not.

"You still have the keys, so go for it."

She didn't look at him.

"Okay, then I'll come back around—"

"I'll drop her off at the Boulderado at four," Todd said.

The man had a different tone to his voice, a gentleness Brice would never have expected. He'd gone from hostile to accepting. Brice was part of their group, and this was Todd's way of telling him.

Brice nodded he was okay with that plan.

Jen watched the logs and reports Vader generated. She saw the type, she didn't register the letters and translate them into words.

Brice wasn't going to spend New Year's in Boulder. He was going back to DC. Back to his life.

He'd given up on her.

She needed to run out of here and confront him about...what? His divorce? About leaving? About staying? About bruising her heart?

"Actually the major does damn fine work, Jennifer."

She looked around to find Todd had rolled his chair right next to hers.

"I didn't think you liked him much."

"I could say the same. But I'd be wrong, wouldn't I? I know it's absolutely none of my business, and I figure you'll tell me to shut up pretty soon, but you seemed pretty happy to be around him."

"Todd, he's a client."

"Sounds like the job is over."

"Aren't we chatty today, Mr. Todd Sargent," Susan said.

Jen was as stunned as Susan. Todd talked in one sentence bites, unless he was presenting evidence, and then the words poured from him. This, right now, was an entire conversation.

"Yes, because I realized he is one of us. I know I'm obsessive to the point of beyond, but he never said a thing. It's who I am, and he didn't get uptight about it. I pushed his buttons because I didn't like losing that case to him. Not because it was him."

The lab was quiet after Todd stopped speaking.

Jen didn't know what to say.

Todd touched her shoulder and rolled his chair back to his station.

Jen still didn't know what to say.

15

RJ WAS PLAYING A JAZZED UP VERSION OF "MOONLIGHT Sonata." The tempo was faster than usual, still melancholy but also bright. Not happy, but mesmerizing.

Brice found two perfect office spaces and wanted to talk to Jen about them, but again worried that she'd feel pressured to run the other direction.

She needed time, not pressure.

He'd ended up at the Boulderado around 2 p.m. and had a beer, then another.

He started watching the door for Jen starting at about three o'clock, and started worrying at five minutes after four.

Then Jen came in on her crutches.

RJ finished playing and got to her before Brice could. He saw the piano man slip an envelope into Jen's hand, then give him a wave before heading back to his keyboard.

Brice finally reached her and guided her to the couch

he'd practically laid claim to for the afternoon. He signaled the bartender, who gave him a thumbs up.

"Here you go. The last of the logs. Like I said, Vader will knock the industry on its heels," Jen said with a bright smile.

Just then a waiter put down a footed champagne bucket in front of them, along with two crystal flutes. Brice nodded for him to go ahead. The cork was popped, the glasses filled.

Brice held up one and clinked it to Jen's.

"To Jennifer Malone. We couldn't have done it without you. Vader and I thank you."

"To Vader and Major Brice Young, retired. May you have all the success in the world."

RJ began playing *Over The Rainbow*. Brice topped off their glasses, and Jennifer drank hers down in nearly a single gulp.

"Listen, I hope you don't mind, but I'm really exhausted. Todd is waiting in the BMW, with Vader tucked safely tucked in the back. He'll take us back to the garage, so he can get his car, and we can go home."

Home, that would be nice. Tomorrow, he'd be back in his dinky little apartment. "Sure that works, let's get you home." He left his full glass on the table.

JEN WATCHED THE CLOCK AS ITS HANDS HIT MIDNIGHT.

Tomorrow was the last day of the year.

New Year's Eve.

Today was just another day.

Liar. It's not another day, it's the day Brice leaves you and goes back to his normally scheduled life.

Not able to sleep, she lay in bed until 4 a.m., then slid her crutches down the stairs and limped down after them. It wasn't easy peeling and chopping with the damn things under her arms, but she got it all done.

Suddenly it was 5 a.m. and Brice entered through the back door.

"I have bacon thawed, and veggies cut if you want an omelet."

"I'd love it. I'll set the table and make the coffee."

As they sat at the table, Jen was reminded of the first time they'd eaten an omelet.

"Yeah, I can't believe it was only six days ago," Brice said, putting down his fork, staring at her intently.

"Mind reading again?"

"How could I not?"

Then read this, come back soon. Please give me a chance.

There was a sharp knock on the door. Jen glanced at the clock and saw it was 6 a.m. The chauffeur was here.

She stood in the driveway as Brice loaded Vader into the back seat along with his laptop and carry-on bag.

Jen swallowed hard, her throat clogged with tears. She knew if she tried to say anything, she'd fail, and the tears she'd tried so hard to choke back would fall.

"Thank you for everything, Jennifer Malone," Brice whispered in her ear. He quickly bussed her lips and pulled her against him, holding her tight. She felt his lips press on her hair.

He got into the limo without another word, and the long sleek car was gone.

She decided to take the day off.

THE REST OF THE DAY WAS PASSING FAR TOO SLOWLY.

She wanted to call Annie and cry on her shoulder, and many times the phone was in her hand to do just that. But she didn't. She wasn't even sure what she'd tell her.

Jen wanted to pace, to scream, but instead she made a nest, lit the fire, and looked at an old photo album filled with scenes of happier times.

Under her graduation picture was Doc's scrawled *Sometimes it takes a leap of faith.*

Right, Doc, I wish you were here to tell me just what that means.

Her home lab drew her and she limped out, not knowing why until she pulled out the sleeper couch to strip off the sheets and found Brice's sweatshirt balled up under the covers.

Jen sat on the edge of the bed, held the shirt to her face and inhaled the scent of Brice. He didn't wear aftershave or cologne, but his soap, shampoo and pure masculinity clung to the fabric.

Then her tears fell hot and fast. She realized she'd been looking at divorce and its aftermath through the eyes of a child. The hurt, the abandonment and even the guilt that she might have been the cause.

Curling up on the couch bed, she let the misery of her

childhood fall away. It was the past and Brice was the future. She needed to understand what caused his divorce, for she realized that he wasn't a man to run away from a mistake. She'd been too wrapped up in her own misery to listen. Sleep claimed her with that thought in her heart.

When she woke, evening had settled in. She took the sweatshirt with her and, once in her kitchen, fixed a cup of cocoa, painfully aware of the last time she'd drunk some. She hobbled to the living room window and stared at the star resting on Flagstaff Mountain.

She could wish all she wanted, but seeing if there was a chance for this relationship to move forward was going to take more than a wish, it was going to take that leap of faith Doc had penned on her picture.

But for once, she didn't know exactly what step to take next.

Give her a keyboard and computer, and she was ready set go. Get her in the witness stand, and she would be cool and precise laying out the facts.

But this? Did she call Brice, tell him that she was jumping a jet and heading to DC? Why not? *Leap of faith, Jen.*

As if she were moved by puppet strings, maybe held in Doc's hands, she pulled out her laptop and looked for flights, but nothing was available. Nothing in time anyway.

And then what would she say once she got there?

Leap of faith, girl. If you love him, and you do, when you do reach him, you have to listen, then find the right words to convince him.

"Fantastic work, Brice," General Cartwright said. "Vader will do phenomenally well. Let me go over the logs tonight, and I'll get back to you tomorrow. By the way, Lilly would love for you to come to dinner New Year's Eve, a small party of a few close friends."

Brice turned from the window and the gray, sullen sky of DC. "General, I'd love to, but I need a huge favor instead."

16

BRICE HAD LED COMBAT TRAINING MISSIONS THAT WEREN'T as terrifying as what he was doing this very moment. Standing outside Jen's house.

He could have completely misjudged Jennifer Malone, and if so, he'd climb back into his rented SUV, drive back to Denver International Airport, and try and find a way to get to Pasadena for tomorrow's parade.

The light was on in her bedroom so she was home and awake. Thankfully it wasn't much past 9 p.m.

He slipped the key in the lock and turned it, thankful he'd forgotten to return it to her. Then opened the door. "Jen? Jen? It's Brice."

Then he realized she still might not be able to walk down the stairs. So he paused at the bottom and looked up.

There she stood, shock written across her face. She had on sweat pants and his Air Force sweatshirt, the one he wore his first day here. How had he missed that when he packed?

"You came back."

"I told you I was going to spend New Year's in Boulder."

She didn't smile. "Can we talk?"

"Sure, want me to come up there?"

"Uh, no, I'll get dressed—"

"No, don't. You look pretty wonderful just like that."

She walked down the stairs gingerly, sans crutches. As they headed toward the living room, he noticed a nest built in front of the fireplace and hoped Jen would head that direction, but she veered toward the kitchen instead.

They sat at the travertine counter, beautiful but cold and hard.

None of this boded well for his plan.

"Listen, what I have to say is best said facing each other, so can we please use the couch?" he asked.

"Nope, too many memories in there. And I have a lot to say as well."

"Then you first."

"Guests first."

He swallowed hard, and tried to remember all he'd planned to say, but couldn't, so Brice spoke from his heart and hoped she'd believe. "I get that you distrust people who have divorced, and sometimes that's warranted, but I truly did make a stupid mistake with Bethany. And she with me.

"I told you a bit of this before, but bear with me. After Bethany's miscarriage, she wanted to try again immediately. I didn't. I had already decided to leave the Air

Force after my twenty and work on Vader. When I told her my decision, she went ballistic and told me that she'd married a general, and damn if I wouldn't stay in and be one.

"I left, got drunk at the officer's club, and a couple of guys from another base asked me how married life was with the "officer bunny." I didn't know that about her, and frankly at that point didn't care. She'd already told me what she'd expected from me. But I also realized that I'd been blinded to anything other than she was really hot for me, or I guess my uniform. I wanted it to work because that's what I thought marriage was all about, working through the issues. But I was wrong. It's about love, first and foremost, and neither of us loved the other.

"Divorce isn't painless, but sometimes it's the right decision. You were screwed, but that was your parents' fault, the people, not the legal document that decrees the divorce."

Jen took it all in, he could see it in her eyes. He just hoped she believed that being divorced wasn't the death knell to another relationship.

It was her turn. He took a deep breath, waiting.

"I realized yesterday that I was looking at all the pain, the disillusionment through a child's viewpoint. And why not? Annie and I were both subjected to the loss of a parent, whether it was physical, when her mother just upped and left them, or in my case that I was ignored by both.

"I dated, but I never felt connected to any of the men. And then this guy and I seemed to be on the right wavelength, until he broke it off saying I was too smart for him and maybe myself. And that it was better to find out now that the relationship was a mistake than get divorced in a year. So yes, I admit I was and still am gun shy, worried that you'll think after a while, for whatever reason, that you've made a mistake with me."

BRICE WANTED NOTHING MORE THAN TO ERASE THAT uncertainty from Jen's eyes and heart. "Thank God that guy was a total idiot."

His line earned him a small smile from Jen. "The only thing I can do is promise that every day I'll do my best to show you just the opposite, that being with you is the best decision I've ever made. And maybe you'll decide that I'm the man for you. That you'll love me as much as I love you."

Jen touched his face, cupping his cheek. She shook her head, but there wasn't sadness in her eyes, it was something like wonderment. Damn, those people that didn't love and cherish her needed to be permanently removed from her memory.

He took her hand and kissed her palm. Hoping someday she'd love him. But right now, he'd take this moment and treasure it.

"Doc told me that sometimes it takes a leap of faith. I think really it's more of taking a first step, and then another. I love you, Brice. And I can't imagine anyone else

I'd rather walk with on this journey through life than you," she said softly.

Enough of the kitchen counter. He pulled her from the stool and crushed her to his chest. Then he kissed her hair smelling the fresh scent of her shampoo. He gently raised her face his finger, and showered her lips, her eyes and her lips again with kisses. Filled with humbleness that Jen was entrusting her heart to him.

He held her away from him for a second and studied her eyes.

"What?"

"It's gone."

"What's gone?"

"All the doubt, all the hurt."

"Yes, it is. Yes, it definitely is."

This time Jen showered his face with butterfly kisses and nips that drove him nearly over the edge.

And then she pulled back, reached for something on the counter and handed him an envelope. The same one he'd seen RJ give her at the Boulderado.

"I got these for us before I knew you were leaving."

He pulled out two tickets to the Boulderado's New Year's Party.

"We still have time if you want to go."

"Shucks, I'd love to."

And received a cuff on the shoulder for his answer.

"Give me five minutes to change."

≈

BRICE DROVE HIS RENTAL AND PARKED IN JEN'S PARKING space. She left her crutches at the house, insisting on wearing her boots, and that her ankle was up for the walk to the Boulderado.

Nevertheless, they strolled slowly down the Pearl Street Mall, enjoying the crowds and the anticipation for a new beginning that filled the air on New Year's Eve.

Suddenly fireworks shot into the sky, brilliant and booming. Brice checked his watch. Midnight on the dot.

"Happy New Year, Miss Jennifer Malone. Will you be forever mine?"

"Happy New Year to you, Major Brice Young, retired. Forever yours sounds pretty darn perfect."

Brice swept her closer, then dipped her for a soul-melding kiss as fireworks filled the sky.

~ The End ~

DEAR READER

Dear Reader,

The Star Light ~ Star Bright series was born after I had a number of readers contact me and tell me they wanted more from the characters they'd met in *Be Mine This Christmas Night*

Incredibly exciting stuff for an author to hear!

Naturally it had to be Jen's story in *Forever Yours This New Year's Night*. Then I developed Brice who both Jen and I adore. And I gave him a sister, who has her own book.

What about Mitch you ask? You know I couldn't leave him miserable, he's really a super nice guy with a lot of love in him, so his book is #3, *Believe In Me This Christmas Morn* and features a new heroine, Belle Grantham. Named after my Aunt Leslie Belle, and Grantham was my grandmother's maiden name.

Brice's sister, Caro, is a spunky sprite and her novella with Maximillian (Max) is #4 in the series, *Dream Of Me This Christmas Eve.*

The characters you've met through out the series including those you meet in Book 4 will be featured in Book 5. When? I don't know, but they are hammering at me to write them. So....

I hope you loved reading Jen and Brice's story as much as I did writing it. If so, please leave a review on the store's review site where you purchased it. And if you can at BookBub and Goodreads as well. We writers live or die by reviews. I know it sounds dramatic but it is so true. Reviews are the way readers find us and buy the book. Without those coveted stars we'd never be chosen out of the millions of choices readers have today.

Also, on my website www.lesliesartor.com, you can find entire *Star Light ~ Star Bright* series on the "Book Shelf" page.

And I have a newsletter that enjoy writing and sending monthly. Keeping you up to date on my writing, my crazy busy life and often my photography. And don't forget, I love hearing from you via email!

ALSO BY L. A. SARTOR

STAR LIGHT ~ STAR BRIGHT

A Romantic Christmas Series Set In Snowy Boulder, Colorado

Be Mine This Christmas Night

Forever Yours This New Year's Night

Believe In Me This Christmas Morn

Dream Of Me This Christmas Eve

THE CARSWELL ADVENTURE SERIES

Heart Pounding Adventure & Romance Set In Exotic Locales

Stone Of Heaven

Viking Gold

THE KAHUNA GROUP

Romantic Suspense With Powerful, Professional Investigators-
Offices in Hawaii ~ Denver ~ Los Angeles

Dare To Believe

Brushed By Betrayal

THE PLANTATION SERIES

Pure Romance Set in Costa Rica On A Rare Cacao Plantation

Prince Of Granola

THE JENNA HART JEWELRY MYSTERIES

A Cozy Mystery Series Set in the Colorado Ski Town Of
Angelcroft

Tick Tock Dead (coming soon)

Capture the code with a mobile device's QR reader to see all
of L.A. Sartor's Books

ACKNOWLEDGMENTS

Audra Harders, who is a stellar author in her own right, for believing in me after I was ready to throw in the towel on creating a series. Thankfully she never lets my pity party last long.

Josh Moulin, who took the time to help me work through just what Brice Young designed and Jennifer Malone had to test. Josh is a digital forensics and cyber security expert that leads a team of cyber security professionals for a United States Federal Agency that has a national security mission. Please visit his website: http://JoshMoulin.com

My Beta Readers, Christine Dunning, Jessie Peiker, Nina Victor and Audra Harders.

My Editor, Ellis Vidler, who, as always, makes me a better writer and story teller.

ABOUT THE AUTHOR

I started writing as a child, really. A few things happened on the way to becoming a published author ... specifically, a junior high school teacher who told me I couldn't write because I didn't want to study grammar.

That English teacher stopped my writing for years. But the muse couldn't be denied, and eventually I wrote, a lot, some of it award winning.

My husband told me repeatedly that independent publishing was becoming a valid way to publish a novel. I didn't believe him. I thought indie meant vanity press.

I couldn't have been more wrong.

I started pursuing this direction seriously, hit the keyboard, learned a litany of new things and published my first novel. My second book became a bestseller, and I'm absolutely on the right course in my life.

I live in Colorado with my husband Gary whom I met on a blind date—I can't imagine life without my best friend. We play in the mountains and travel as much as possible.

Find me at www.lesliesartor.com

BELIEVE IN ME THIS CHRISTMAS MORN

STAR LIGHT ~ STAR BRIGHT SERIES BOOK THREE

1

"UNCLE MITCH, I WISH YOU WERE COMING TOO," PETER Evans whispered.

Mitchell Thomas hid his smile, quite sure that his nephew had no idea just how awkward an uncle coming along on a honeymoon would be.

Glancing toward the newly created family waiting for Peter on the curb under the awning at Denver International Airport, Mitch acknowledged the pain that was always present, but more so today. Cole, his brother-in-law, wrapped his arm around his wife of a few hours, Annie Hamilton-Evans, and Annie wrapped her arm around Josh, Cole's younger son and Mitch's other nephew.

Mitch took a breath and pushed away the feeling of now being a fifth wheel in the family. "How about you bring me home a shell, the prettiest one you can find," he said, not wanting to make Peter feel bad about going to Hawaii.

"Deal," the boy said.

Mitch wrapped him in a quick goodbye hug, then watched as his nephew ran to the curb, and Annie came to the SUV to get the last bag, a huge carry-on filled with what, he couldn't imagine. Probably stuff to keep the boys occupied on the long flight to Hawaii.

Mitch handed her the bag.

"Thanks for bringing us to the airport," Annie said, hefting the carry-on to her shoulder. "I know today was hard for you, and I was pretty sure you wanted to be anywhere but around us for another hour or so, yet you offered to bring us to the airport."

"I had to be here anyway, so it all worked out."

Mitch braved Annie's searching look, knowing she was thinking *yeah, right. Stop fooling around with me.* She was a hard woman to fool. "You're getting covered in the white stuff." He forced a smile, trying to keep the conversation light.

"Doesn't matter. Did you know that even before the wedding, the boys wondered if you'd be okay today? Josh was pretty darn worried about you. And Peter wanted you to walk me down the aisle instead of him."

His two nephews meant everything to him, and to know they were thinking about him at all today made his cheek muscles relax into a genuine smile.

"I'm fine. Really. Enjoy the islands. It will be a different kind of honeymoon, but I'm glad you're making the boys a part of it."

"You know Cole and I wouldn't have it any other way.

Last night Pete asked about how 'my first mom' might be feeling about this. And I've got to admit, for once I didn't have an answer that sounded right."

Mitch pushed away the pang of sorrow that still snagged his heart even though Lauren had been dead three years. The reality was that his sister was gone and his nephews couldn't do any better than have Annie as their stepmom. "First and foremost, Lauren would have wanted the boys to be happy and secure. That's what I told him when he asked me."

This time his smile wasn't forced as Annie's eyebrows shot toward her hairline.

From the corner of his eye Mitch saw Cole, still on the curb, waving his finger in a circle, indicating it was time to wrap this up and get Annie moving.

"Go, Cole looks like he needs you. Have a safe flight."

"You, too. By the way, I think the website contest was a cool idea, the winner is really lucky to get you."

Annie stood on her tippy toes, and Mitch bent to receive her kiss on the cheek. Then he watched as she hurried to her new family. The foursome turned around to wave goodbye, then headed inside the terminal.

Another zing to his heart. He heard himself sigh and hated how lonely he felt at this moment.

Mitch got back into his new Lexus and headed toward the airport's parking lot. He wasn't going to be gone more than a couple of days max, working on the website of his contest winner. So he picked the close-in parking, figuring the cost wouldn't be outrageous for that short time. And with amazing luck, he got a space on his first time around the maze of the multistoried parking structure.

After entering DIA's terminal, a two-hour delay greeted him at the departure board, lengthened from the hour he'd seen when he checked the flight status on his phone before leaving Boulder.

Mitch didn't want another drink after all the glasses of champagne at the wedding reception, but he didn't want coffee either. So he headed for the ice cream shop in the main terminal, thinking about his nephews and their love of ice cream, on any day, in any weather.

They took after Lauren. But while they and Lauren loved anything with the word chocolate in it, he was partial to anything with nuts and caramel.

Sitting in front of his double-scoop bowl of caramel nut cluster with, in honor of the boys, a healthy dose of hot fudge on top, he dug in. Savoring the mix of flavors, he tried to focus on the website needs of his contest winner before their up-coming meeting.

Belle Grantham currently lived in Pagosa Springs, Colorado, and had won his contest. The prize was that he'd create a website for the winner and maintain it for a year. Her nonprofit literacy project, Goal 100% ~ Literacy for Women, was in desperate need of a boost.

Yep, she needed him. Mitch's website company was tops in the industry. He could pick and choose his clients, something that still blew his mind. Eleven years ago, he'd barely made ends meet in expensive Denver when he'd left Web Wizards and decided to go solo, creating his own company, It's Alive Web Design.

Mitch glanced at his phone clock and realized he'd been sitting for over an hour in front of a whistle-clean ice cream bowl. He'd better head for the gate. This season, a week before Christmas, security wasn't speedy even in the TSA pre-qualified line. By the time he got to the gate, they were calling his row to board. Onward to Durango, Colorado, to pick up his rental car, drive the sixty miles to Pagosa Springs, and meet Belle Grantham.

THE AIRPORT IN DURANGO WASN'T LARGE, AND THERE WERE only a few flights to this Western-slope Colorado town throughout the day. Nevertheless, Belle's palms were moist with fear that she'd miss connecting with Mitchell Thomas before he left the terminal to drive to Pagosa Springs.

The paper sign she'd carefully printed in bold letters with his name was wilting where she clutched it. She shouldn't be the least bit worried—after all, this could be an important detour, and she was sure Mitchell would understand once she told him. Belle knew what she was proposing wasn't like asking him to fly to the moon, but neither did she want to alienate him. She knew Goal 100% desperately needed a new website.

Which would translate to *a lot* more donations. Belle couldn't, wouldn't, allow her baby to go belly up. But the harsh reality was that she couldn't afford to continue much longer as things stood at the moment.

So when one of her board members, Armstrong

Worth, or Armie to a select few, said he needed to meet with her about a large donation, she jumped at the chance. As he was her oldest friend, she was delighted to meet with him.

She just didn't want to do this right now and have her attention divided. She'd wanted to focus singularly on Mitchell Thomas's website ideas.

Belle let loose a soft, tired sigh, realizing just how bone-weary she really was. Goal 100% was a one-woman operation. Sure she had volunteers running the centers and doing the tutoring, but it was all on her to do everything else. Fund-raising, office work, flying out to train the tutors, print the materials. The list really was endless.

Yet it was the passion of her life. She needed more money to bring in some help, even part time. Thus the importance of keeping Mitchell Thomas happy.

As the first of the passengers exited the security area, Belle bucked up, pasted on a bright smile, and held the sign high.

"I'm Mitchell Thomas," a deep voice said from her right.

She turned to look at the tall man in front of her, and her mouth suddenly felt full of hot, dry rocks.

She'd expected a nerd. The man in front of her wasn't anything like the picture on his own website. While she was all of five-feet-nine inches, Mitchell stood at least three inches taller. And damn if he wasn't tripping her switches with the slight cleft in his five o'clock-shaded chin.

In his photograph, he'd worn black-rimmed glasses. Now, sans the frames, his electric blue eyes studied her with an intensity that slightly unnerved her. An unusual position for her to be in.

Basically, she realized, he didn't look the type of person to be led around and cajoled as she was going to have to do to get him back on a plane.

She'd miscalculated big time. "Belle Grantham—"

"Yes, I know."

She blinked, taken aback again. Belle hastily released one side of the paper to wipe her damp palm on her jeans, then stuck her hand out in greeting.

Mitchell grasped it in a firm, single shake and released it. He tilted his head just a tad as if to study her.

"I saw your picture on your website, which by the way, doesn't do you justice. But we'll fix that. What I don't know is what you're doing here. Aren't I supposed to be meeting with you in Pagosa Springs for the next couple of days? Did you decide to be my chauffeur?"

Belle swallowed hard. What she was about to tell Mitchell had all sounded so simple when Armie had proposed his plan to her over the phone a few hours ago.

Now it sounded impossible.

"I needed to catch you before you left the airport." Belle forced herself to maintain eye contact with him for the bombshell she was going to drop. "I have to catch the last flight to Denver." She glanced at the clock on the wall above her. "Which leaves in about twenty minutes. They've already started the boarding call."

Belle bit her lower lip as she watched his brows arch in

surprise, then furrow in worry above those damn fine eyes in the span of a few seconds. The first emotion she could understand, but why the look of worry? Unless he hated to fly.

Uh-oh.

Or maybe it was anger that made his brows come together over his nose.

Double uh-oh. Not a good way to start this crucial business relationship.

"You want me to fly back to Denver?"

"I already have our tickets. We just need to go through security again. I can explain it on the way," she said, rushing her words, feeling less and less in control.

"How about explaining the pertinent points now? The flight over was horrible with the weather. Is this a family crisis?"

He raised a brow, waiting for her answer, and Belle knew instinctively nothing but the truth would do. "No, thankfully it's not family per se. Have you heard of Armstrong Worth?" She expected a nod and received it. Nearly anyone who watched any news feed or broadcast knew of Armie.

To Belle he was simply the guy she went to elementary school with back in the Hill Country of Texas. Then on to private secondary school, each telling their parents they'd quit school if they couldn't go to the same one.

He was the boy—almost man—of eighteen, who escorted her to her debutante ball and the one who splashed her unmercifully in the pool at her papa's Trickle Creek ranch, or his dad's Circle W Doubled ranch.

"Well, Armie is a close friend and he's on the board of my nonprofit." Belle continued her explanation to Mitchell and watched his nod. Of course he'd known—it would make sense that he'd done research on her and the nonprofit.

"He specifically changed his travel plans to a huge economic summit in London to make a short layover at DIA, of course not checking with me first. But he did this so he could meet with me about Goal 100% once he learned..." She trailed off and shied away from looking directly at Mitchell's piercing blue eyes.

"Go on, I don't bite," he said, then smiled as if to make his point.

Mitchell was wrong about the biting. He had the whitest, strongest teeth she'd ever see. And at the country club near Austin, near where she grew up and where everyone whitened and straightened, that was saying something.

"Once he learned that Goal 100% was nearly broke."

MITCH RUBBED HIS CHIN, FEELING THE ROUGHNESS OF HIS five o'clock shadow. He bit down on his frustration at having his carefully wrought plans thrown to the wind all because of a rich guy who crooked his little finger. The last thing he wanted to do was head back to Denver and then Boulder and the memories he was escaping. "You've got a powerful guy on your side. But why does he need to meet with you? Why can't he just have this discussion via phone?"

Just then the intercom blasted the last boarding call for the flight to Denver. Mitch glanced at Belle.

A touch of panic flared in her eyes. "Mitchell, I know this is a huge inconvenience. But this meeting may be as important to me as winning your contest. Together, a new website and what I'm hoping could be an infusion of cash could really make the nonprofit viable until it gets legs and becomes huge. And I figured we could work in your neck of the woods as easily as mine."

Yeah, but I don't want to be in my neck of the woods, Ms. Belle Grantham.

Mitch, fighting his frustration, looked over Belle's head as the last of his fellow passengers exited out of the security area into the terminal. He didn't relish getting back on an airplane, but if she really needed to see this guy and wasn't going to be around to help him, the point of his being here was moot.

"Let's go."

Belle smiled with relief, and unexpectedly his irritation over the high-handedness of Armstrong Worth's tactics fled. Her eyes turned from hazel to almost emerald in color. Dimples appeared in her cheeks, and she was simply gorgeous.

Mitch looked at her more closely.

She wore a black cashmere sweater, jeans that looked distressed but he bet cost a fortune, black knee-high boots, and a pale lavender ski parka that boasted a fancy name.

Her clothes alone were the cost of a first class airplane ticket to...Hawaii.

Her deep auburn hair, cut in a sleek bob that ended just below her chin, swung like rippling satin as she bent down and hoisted a huge leather satchel over one shoulder.

He hadn't noticed the bag sitting on the floor next to her or he'd have offered to carry it for her. *What was it with women and their huge satchels?* A slight grin curved his lips upward.

Belle cocked her head, questioning the reason for his smile, and he refused the invitation to tell her. She led the way to security. They were the only two people in line, so it took but a minute to go through the checkpoint.

The gate was close enough to fast-walk—even so, they were the last passengers to board the small jet. Luckily the flight was only partially filled, so they had their choice of seats. Belle led the way to the back and took the last row, away from the other handful of passengers.

They belted in, taxied, and in minutes were climbing through the clouds and the unrelenting snow. The jet shuddered a bit, did a belly-dropping bump, and then leveled out.

Belle clutched the armrests so tightly her knuckles really were white. He reached across the short space between them and touched her hand. "Are you going to be okay?"

"I'm not the best flier. Or at least not on these small jets," she admitted. "If we don't have any more of those sickening drops, I'll be fine. Thanks for asking."

Mitch pitied her wan smile. He didn't like this kind of flying either, but thought of it as inconvenient rather than defying death.

"Oh,"—Belle interrupted his thoughts—"I forgot to mention that Armie said he'll reimburse you for your flight over to Durango, and of course he paid for these tickets."

Nope. No way in hell was Mitch going to take a dime from "Armie" Worth. "Thanks, but I don't need him to reimburse me for anything." He watched in slight amusement as Belle's brow furrowed and her mouth opened, then shut. He wasn't going to argue this point. Additionally, he'd figure out a way for "Armie" to get his money back for this flight's ticket as well. After all, a guy had his pride.

"However," Mitch continued. "I am surprised that Goal 100% is nearly broke. Your spreadsheet listed only a few expenses, and it didn't look financially unsound. You have a regular, dependable donation coming in each month, although I'm not sure how that person got through the donation process on your website. I tried, but I couldn't get through the screens and gave up.

"Cleaning up your website should help in a big way. It *is* pretty awful. It's bland, doesn't inspire confidence, and lacks a singular focus."

The minute those words left his mouth, he cringed inwardly, wanting to stuff them back in his mouth. God, he was a pain in the ass at times.

"Wow, is that all that's wrong with it?"

But instead of the woman sitting next to him

appearing to be thunderously mad over his foot-in-mouth statement, she laughed. A clear, lovely sound. Not haughty or imperious, which was what he'd expected after learning more about her once she'd won the contest.

For Belle Grantham was pretty simple to sum up. She was a Texas Hill Country, mega-ranch, rich girl. She was Country Club, had made her debut in the traditional formal way, and gone to Wellesley.

She was everything he wasn't.

Yet her concept of the nonprofit Goal 100%~Literacy for Women touched a chord inside him. The cause was something both he and Lauren vehemently believed in.

"That's why I was so pleased to win your contest. As I thought Armie, Papa, and my brother would be. Papa and Junior make up the rest of the board of Goal 100%."

He knew that but figured he'd said enough for the time being.

Belle picked at the leather on the armrest, looked out the window, and finally at him. "The fund looks like it's in the black because I've been the one making that regular donation from my trust fund. This way, all the other donations go to the literacy centers that are up and running. I add the extra money that's needed to fill the gaps."

Mitch couldn't believe what he was hearing. Belle was using her own money to keep the nonprofit afloat?

"I live pretty simply in the Pagosa Springs ranch house the family uses for summer vacations, and the rent on the office space, as you know since you studied my spreadsheet, is nominal. Nevertheless, the real donations are small, pitifully small."

That he could help with. But he was still stuck on the fact that she funded her own nonprofit and did the work of an entire staff. He felt a tiny bit of the stereotype of a rich county-club girl he held against her evaporate.

He focused back on Belle's words.

"But they, as the board, have apparently realized that I'm funding the nonprofit and that it's a pretty shaky endeavor. I get that. I never intended to always use my trust fund. Frankly I thought the donations would be handling all the expenses now. The board has been making subtle hints about changing things, which is why I'm so grateful you chose me as your winner. I just need more time."

Her green eyes took on a militant look, and Mitch chuckled inwardly, figuring Belle wasn't someone to cross.

The jet did another stomach-flopping drop. "God, I hate flying in these planes. I'm going to make Armie bump up his donation just for that reason alone."

Laughter burst from Mitch's lips. After they got done meeting with Worth, Mitch knew the next few days working with Belle would be more interesting than the hours spent with most of his clients.

Which reminded him that he needed to call and cancel his reservations at the hotel right next to Pagosa Springs's famous hot springs. He'd been interested in trying the various thermal pools at differing temperatures but figured it could hold for another time.

A second later he realized that Belle would need a place to stay for the duration of their work, and it obviously couldn't be with him. It would be totally inappropriate for him to host a client.

And the fact that she's a stunning woman has nothing to do with it, right?

Of course. It's simply a matter of no room at the Inn.

Liar.